about the author

Norman Silver was born in Cape Town, South Africa, in 1946. He read Philosophy at the University of the Witwatersrand and in 1969 moved to England to further his studies.

But the cultural shock of his new life produced radical changes in his thinking, particularly with regard to South Africa and racial issues. He abandoned his studies in order to explore alternative ideas and lifestyles.

He worked in remand homes for adolescents in London and Bristol, and taught computer programming in Ipswich until 1987, when he fulfilled a lifelong desire to take up writing full time. *No Tigers in Africa* was the first result. He also writes poetry and his debut collection for teenagers *Words on a Faded T-Shirt* was published in 1991 at the same time as a collection of South African-based short stories — *An Eye for Colour*. *Python Dance,* a novel and the third volume in this 'South African trilogy', followed in 1992.

Norman Silver is married with two teenage children. His wife is a clinical psychologist. They live in Suffolk.

An Eye For Colour

NORMAN SILVER

faber and faber

LONDON · BOSTON

First published in 1991
by Faber and Faber Limited
3 Queen Square London WC1N 3AU
This paperback edition first published in 1992

Printed in England by Clays Ltd, St Ives plc

© Norman Silver, 1991

Norman Silver is hereby identified as the author of this work
in accordance with Section 77 of the Copyright, Designs and
Patents Act 1988.

A CIP record for this book is available
from the British Library

ISBN 0–571–16779–9

2 4 6 8 10 9 7 5 3 1

Contents

Fifty-fifty tutti-frutti chocolate-chip

I'm sure the nicest ice-cream in the whole world comes from Napoli. If you're ever in Sea Point you must try it. They do a fifty-fifty tutti-frutti chocolate-chip with almond topping that does full justice to God's creation of a tongue. Somehow that particular ice-cream sets off every taste-bud on your tongue with a rhythm of sensations that you won't get anywhere else, I'm sure of it.

That Napoli restaurant won't mind me advertising them, because for a month, while I was holidaying at my grandparents' flat in Sea Point, I was a regular customer there. Every night, about half-past eleven, I'd arrive there for my treat. After the first week, I didn't even have to say what I wanted.

'Good evening, sir. Two fifty-fifty tutti-frutti chocolate-chips with almond topping?'

After that, the walk from Napoli to Green Point was delicious, with this ice-cream cone in my hand, and the taste-bud music popping on my tongue.

Of course, holding hands with Sandra while we walked was nice, too. Especially as she had this neat habit of softly rubbing the palm of my hand with her thumb.

Mind you, I've always fancied ice-creams. When I was a kid my dad and ma used to take me out on these weekend picnics, to Hout Bay or Camps Bay, or the Strand, or Stellenbosch, or Paarl. We would drive for miles to find the right place to picnic. I didn't mind a bit, because I knew they'd buy me a rainbow ice-cream when we stopped.

My dad and ma used to sing all these songs as we drove along like 'Row, row, row your boat, gently down the stream, merrily, merrily, merrily, merrily, life is but a dream'. However, the dream had begun long ago to fade into reality as my parents and me clashed more and more about everything, and in particular about choosing a decent career for myself.

I've always been interested in journalism, but my dad and ma had other ideas. On my fourteenth birthday they surprised me with this present of a book called *The Miracle of the Human Body*. It came complete with colourful transparencies, so that across the white bones of the skeleton you could overlay pictures of the muscles, or the blood vessels, or the vital organs, or the nervous system, etc. etc.

I couldn't see myself why this book should have any interest for me, particularly as seeing blood wasn't my speciality, but the inscription on the inside cover made it perfectly clear: 'To our dear son Basil, the future doctor (or surgeon, or specialist), may this book help you on your way to a dedicated career devoted to helping others, from Popidoo and Momidoo.'

That was a monumental day in my life, because not only was the book heavy as hell, but I could feel the pressure from my parents was also as heavy as hell.

For a while I tried every possible tactic to accidentally destroy this book and my parents' plans for my future. I dumped it in the garbage bin by accident; I put it in a cardboard box of clothes which my mother was giving to charity. But the book was miraculous in more than just name. Each time it returned from the dead.

Once I even took it with me on a weekend to relations in Mossel Bay and accidentally left it behind when we returned to Cape Town. But a month later it arrived, wrapped in brown paper, with a note from my aunt explaining that her servant girl, Eileen, had found it stuck behind the wardrobe in the room where I had slept. She felt obliged to post it back to me because she knew how much I must be missing it.

In the end I decided to ceremonially burn the book one afternoon in our braaivleis in the backyard. (My dad made that braaivleis from a metal barrel, which he found somewhere; he sawed it in half and attached a wire grill across the open hole.) I can tell you that it took a lot of guts to burn that book on the altar which my dad had constructed with his own hands. As the flames leapt into action, doing their mysterious dance of death on each of the one thousand three hundred and eighty-nine curling pages of that book, my heart also was doing its mysterious dance of breaking free from my parents' control.

When it came to Sunday lunch-time and my dad began to prepare the fire, a half-burnt image of the large intestines stared up at him from the ashes in the bottom of the barrel. You could clearly read that it was page 743, but even so, I was surprised that my dad made the connection as quickly as he did. After all, how could he have guessed my murderous intentions towards that book? He was furious.

'That book cost fifty-something rands! You've burnt to ashes a good career.'

Thereafter, steaks grilled on that braai didn't taste so good; it was as if the burnt picture of the large intestines hovered like a ghoul at the spot where the book had been sacrificed.

But I needed to make that statement about the direction of my own life. That was also the reason why I chose to go on holiday on my own to Sea Point that summer. I know it wasn't much of a distance from our house in Claremont to Sea Point – it was only two bus rides away – but at least it was one means of getting a break from my parents' nagging. For a while they tried to force me to take my young brother Ivan with me. That would have spoiled everything! Imagine having to drag around a nine-year-old wherever I went!

No, my parents would have to get used to the idea that I was an independent person and almost an adult. And when I met Sandra on that holiday, I reckoned my folks would also have to get used to the idea that I was capable of having a serious and mature relationship with a girl.

When I used to drop Sandra off at her house in Green Point, I would give her a final goodnight kiss tasting of fifty-fifty tutti-frutti chocolate-chip Napoli ice-cream, and arrange to meet her the next day.

Then I'd run all the way back to my grandparents' flat in Sea Point. Actually it wasn't real running. It was more like what you do in some dreams, when you suddenly find that if you tilt your body horizontal to the ground, you are able to fly just by small movements of your hands. It was a sensational feeling! My running steps each seemed to take me about five metres, and I felt so light as I ran along the seafront like that, hardly noticing any of the people who were still promenading up and down in the moonlight.

I suppose I still couldn't believe that Sandra actually liked me so much, and was making herself so available to me, with her deep kisses and intimate cuddles. After all, she was a good looker.

Of course, being after midnight, it was mostly couples promenading, and doing a few other things, too, in the shadows or behind walls. In the daytime and early evening, the seafront belonged to the crowds of old folk and families. And my grandparents were among them.

Everyone knew my grandparents. You could tell them a mile off by the way they walked, with my grandmother leaning heavily on my grandfather's shoulder, and dragging her stiff, artificial leg along as best she could. It never bent properly, that was the problem, and it took her ages to sit down on a bench to rest. So many people stopped to talk to her; everyone loved her, I think, with her warm personality. And although my grandfather maintained that the amputation of her leg had been unnecessary, a medical error of some sort, my grandmother always said she was grateful at least to be mobile. There were so many people, she said, who were too ill or handicapped to be able to enjoy the pleasure of the seafront. (But to tell the truth, in the privacy of her own flat, I used to see her crying sometimes, feeling sorry for herself. Who could blame her, though?)

Most of the summer the seafront had a leisurely, holiday atmosphere. But every New Year the place went wild, especially at night. Local residents had made complaints every year to the police, but still nothing had been done to prevent drunk revellers from rampaging through the streets and kicking up a rumpus right through till the early hours of morning.

Sandra and me spent a quiet New Year's Day together alone on a crowded beach, sharing our affections and resolutions. One of the things I resolved was to pursue the career of journalism in the face of all opposition.

It wasn't only my parents who felt I should not be a journalist. This one teacher, Bonzo, gave us hundreds of aptitude tests and guess what conclusion he came to? He came up with this brilliant suggestion of me taking up accountancy. Me! Such a sensitive person with insight into the human condition! Me! An accountant? I told old Bonzo that he didn't know his arse from his elbow.

This assessment of his ability didn't go down too well, and he gave me the option of rubber tyre or cricket bat.

Bonzo was into violence in a big way. He had this mildly annoying habit of walking around the classroom while we were all concentrating on filling in questionnaires or something. The room would be deadly quiet, but then, with an amused smile on his lips, he would raise his hand to shoulder height and bring it down with full force on some unsuspecting back. The surprise alone, never mind the searing pain, could have killed a boy with a weak heart, but fortunately there weren't any in our class. The handprint would remain on the victim's back for several hours afterwards.

He also had a collection of weapons in the storeroom behind the class which he used with regularity to educate our backsides. There were a dozen canes of varying thicknesses and lengths, cricket bats, tennis rackets, hockey sticks, rubber hoses, pieces of rubber tyre nailed to handles, ropes, lengths of electric cord, and, of course, planks of varying thicknesses and suppleness. I personally think he chose the wrong career for himself: instead of being a teacher at a crappy Cape Town high school, he should have entered the police force.

With regard to the punishment, I was lucky. Although the rubber tyre had a painful reputation, the cricket bat was known as one of the softer options. Also, it was a well-established fact that every night Bonzo looked too deep in the bottle, and therefore didn't use as much force in the mornings, because he didn't like to jolt his hangovered head.

In spite of that, the beating put me right off choosing any career, and I decided to look into the possibilities of becoming a professional surf-bum.

However, that was just an idle fantasy: for one thing, I didn't know how to use a surfboard; for another, my skin tends to go a painful red in the sun.

But it was worth the sunburn, sitting there the whole day on the beach with Sandra, only occasionally getting up to swim in the breakers or to play beach tennis with each other. We made a wonderful twosome.

We used to spend most evenings in Sea Point. And this one particular evening after New Year, wherever we walked there were all these coloured Coons, (or are we supposed to call them Minstrels nowadays?) left over from the day's Carnival, hanging round in twos and threes, dressed up in their satiny costumes, all turquoise and pink

6

and brown and white and green and yellow, playing their lively tambourines and banjos and saxophones and singing 'Dis die Nuwejaar en ons is bymekaar, Bokkie jy moet huis toe gaan.'

I liked the look of those Coons. Their colours were just like the colours of the fifty-fifty tutti-frutti chocolate-chip Napoli ice-creams that were dripping over our hands as we licked them and listened to the music. When they held out their satiny hats, I gave them a few coins for singing and harmonizing so well.

It was easily worth the money, because on the way back to Green Point that night, Sandra and I sang their song that it was the New Year and we were together and it was time for Bokkie to go home. After that I called Sandra 'Bokkie' for the rest of the month.

Then I did my usual flying-running past the seafront on my way home.

But that night I had to crash-land suddenly, because there was a hell of a fight going on. I must have had my head so brightly lit with the memory of Sandra's cuddliness that I forgot to avoid the seafront which I should have known would be wild.

These five white blokes were beating up these two Coons. One white bloke was using a banjo as a lethal weapon, striking the Coons repeatedly with it, and yelling 'Hey darling! Here you are darling!' with each blow he struck.

A group of white girls were huddled by this one bench, drinking out of beer bottles, watching the fight and apparently giggling.

I tell you, those white blokes were cross about something. They kept kicking the Coons in their guts and in their backsides and any other part of their bodies that lay open to attack.

'You don't ever call a white chick "Darling". Verstaan! I

7

don't care if it's bladdy New Year. You stick to your own kind!'

Eventually, when their violence blew out like a candle, they rejoined the girls and stood round for a while drinking and throwing their empty bottles on to the outcrops of rocks. One of the blokes urinated at the side of the pavement before they all continued their promenading up the beach, with their arms around the tight-jeanned back-sides of the girls. The tallest chap thumped the roof of every parked car he passed with his heavy fist. I'm sure their owners must have been very overjoyed in the morning to find their cars suffering from hangovers.

The banjo had been thrown on to the beach sand and it lay there like a monument, gleaming in the broken moon-light.

I remember when I used to go fishing with my dad on rocky outcrops, I used to find these shattered pieces of bottle-glass lying everywhere and I always used to wonder who filthed those places. Now I knew!

Violence has always upset me a lot, but as I stood there keeping my distance and deciding what to do, it occurred to me that what I had just witnessed should be turned into a penetrating article for a newspaper or a magazine.

I had to do something. I walked on to the soft sand and picked up the banjo. Its white circular skin was torn, and some strings were broken. The metal bits were also bent and dented, and the long arm that sticks out was deformed. It was one hell of a mess.

I took it across to the two Coons. They were even more torn and broken and bent and dented than the banjo, I think. Blood was running out of the one man's nose, and his hair was also matted with blood. I could hardly look at him, though I wished I could help him.

'Eina! Eina! Ag, Ma, ek'seer!'

He kept calling for his ma, and rubbing his bloody head with his hand. But at least he was going to survive. It was

8

the other bloke who looked really bad. I couldn't see much
blood on him, but he was just lying there immobilized on
the concrete; the shape of his body didn't look too good.

'Here's your banjo,' I said to the one who was moaning.
'It's broken but maybe you can get it fixed.'

'But how can I get fixed?' he asked me. 'My life pains me
too much.'

I felt terrible standing there. I wanted to do something. I
wanted, at least, to tell them that at that moment I wasn't
too proud of being white.

There are some things you can never say. I remember
when those weekend drives we used to go on turned into
arguments between my ma and dad, about where to picnic,
and most of the journey would be spent on arguing. Then a
gloom would set in, and the journey would be silent for
hour after hour, and they wouldn't find a picnic place that
suited both of them. I sat in the back of that car and
somehow I knew that I couldn't say anything to my
parents.

I felt like screaming for them to stop, but I sat in silence.
Eventually they'd stop somewhere and buy me a rainbow
ice-cream to make *me* feel better at least, but they would just
continue their arguing.

I couldn't think of anything to say to that injured
coloured, so I just tried to help him get up. Leaning on me,
he managed to drag himself to the bench. The second
coloured was lights out.

'You guys stay here!' I said to the one on the bench,
though I don't know how I expected either of them to move
in their condition. 'I'll go and get help for you.'

As I ran the few blocks to my grandparents' flat, I began
to shape in my head the article I would write about racial
violence. The thought of becoming a journalist exhilarated
me. If only I could persuade my parents. But then I
remembered the look of shock on my ma's face, the time I
told her that I was considering taking up journalism.

'Go ahead and do whatever you want,' she generously said. 'It's your decision. If you're not interested in Medical School, what does my opinion matter? I'm only your mother.'

My dad had been equally generous.

'So be a reporter for some lousy newspaper! You'll either end up a poor white, or you'll end up in prison.'

I was pleased one day, though, when my dad met a bloke who was a journalist, albeit for the *Farmer's Weekly* or some other japie magazine. Their antagonism towards my choice of career was slightly lessened when this fellow explained that the money wasn't too bad if you got a good training and made the right contacts.

But I'll tell you the truth: money never meant that much to me. We used to have this board game called Careers, in which you have to choose a certain proportion of three things and then achieve it in your lifetime. The three things were money, fame and happiness. I was such a sucker at the time, (can you believe it?), I used to opt for 100 per cent happiness. Nobody could win playing the game that way, and of course now I'd go for a sensible mix of all three. People used to think I was such a sap choosing 100 per cent happiness, and it's probably not surprising that I never ever won a single game of Careers. That was in itself quite frustrating, because no one likes to play a game without ever winning, do they?

Quite recently I met this girl Janine, and she told me that she divides the world into winners and losers and that she only goes out with blokes who are winners. It's really odd, because even though I've changed a lot since I used to play Careers, she still wouldn't go out with me, even though *I* thought we'd get on like a house on fire.

I was out of breath when I reached the flat. I quietly let myself in with the key. My grandparents were both asleep but woke when they heard me phoning for an ambulance.

'Are you alright, Basil?' my grandmother shouted out

from her bed. 'Who needs an ambulance? Is Sandra hurt, God forbid?'

I went into their bedroom to reassure them that Sandra and me were both okay. Their room had a smell of old people, slightly medicinal, and my grandmother's artificial leg stood in its shoe leaning up against a chair near her bed.

'There's two blokes hurt on the promenade,' I said. 'They need to get to the hospital.'

'Don't go back there, Basil!' my grandmother said. 'You'll get into trouble. There's meshugena people out there.'

'It's alright,' I said. 'I'll only be five minutes.'

I ran out of the flat and down to the bench on the seafront, but the two injured Coons were nowhere to be seen. I knew I was at the right place because of the bench and because the puddle of urine was still there at the side of the pavement. But there was no signs of the Coons! Even the damaged banjo had been taken off somewhere.

The next day, when I told Sandra what had happened, she said those coloureds were probably looking for trouble and that's why they got beaten up.

'Hey, Bokkie! Don't say such things!'

The rest of my holiday, Sandra and me tried to get really close to each other. My grandmother made the best picnic lunches ever – like cold chicken, potato latkes and water-melon – and Sandra and me spent the long sun-drenched days in each other's company, enjoying the beach and the waves and each other's fondness.

But in the last week we started arguing about where to go for our picnics, and she said she had never been too fond of fifty-fifty tutti-frutti chocolate-chip Napoli ice-creams, and that it was much better to keep the flavours separate. (She also mentioned that my squint got on her nerves.) I decided then to take Bokkie home for the last time, and I never saw her again.

Later, I did send my article about the beating up of the Coons to a newspaper, but they didn't accept it. It was returned with a brief note explaining that if I ever came across a newsworthy story I should contact the paper so that one of their reporters could come round to get the details.

Since then I've gone off journalism. It strikes me as something for which you really need dedication. It is something you have to be prepared to go to prison for. And I don't really know if I've got those sorts of ideals.

So what am I going to do instead for a career? My final choice seemed so natural in the end, so right, so easy, as if I'd been destined all along to make this decision.

I'll give you a moment to guess what I'm going to do. I only decided quite recently.

I think it's the perfect choice.

I have decided to go to Medical School.

That's right, I've decided I want to be a doctor. And not just an ordinary doctor. No, I intend to specialize in psychiatry, because I feel I have a lot of insight into how people's minds work. I can see through hypocrisy and the games people play and get right down to the very centre of what makes people tick.

So in a few years time, you'll see me qualifying as a psychiatrist, just you wait. And that surely proves the inaccuracy of Bonzo's aptitude tests, and at the same time it proves the wisdom and foresight of parents, doesn't it? They always knew I'd be a doctor. I tell you, they were so over the moon, they promised they'd buy me a car at the end of my first year at Medical School.

I am convinced a medical career is the perfect choice for me. I always wanted to dedicate and devote myself to other people. And if I make money in the process and become wealthy and famous, well, that's part of winning the Career's game, isn't it?

Loquat tree

You'll never guess who I bumped into the other night.

It was Wendy Rudnik!

After all these years. There she was in the Spur drinking coffee at a table with another girl. I hardly recognized her, but the thing that confirmed it was Wendy, was her classiness. She was dressed immaculately; but she was the sort of girl who couldn't have hidden her elegance and ladylike manners even if she had dressed in sackcloth.

As I ordered my own coffee, my first thought was, would she remember who I was? My second thought was, should I go and say hello to her? What if she didn't recognize me? Or more likely, what if she did recognize me, but pretended not to?

Wendy Rudnik! I couldn't believe it. She used to live in the house diagonally behind us.

The Rudnik's back garden and our backyard touched only at one corner where they shared the fencepost. I think even that one contact was painful for the Rudnik property. Our family had nothing in common with the Rudniks; they were so rich, and I used to think the Rudnik kids were the luckiest kids in the world.

There were three of them: Peter was the oldest; then came Wendy; and the little one was called Oz – he was a similar age to my younger brother, Ivan. I remember thinking that their parents must have only ever read the first page of *Peter Pan*, because otherwise why did they run out of names from that story, and start looking over the rainbow?

Our backyard was small, whereas the Rudnik's back garden was more like a golfcourse. Their acres of grass sloped up towards their double-storeyed mansion without a weed anywhere to be seen. That was all thanks to Amos, the garden boy. He seemed to spend every minute of his life digging out those weeds, and rolling that grass with a heavy roller.

The lawn led up to the tennis court and beyond that to the sparkling swimming pool and the patio where their mom in her bikini and dark glasses and high stiletto heels used to come stretch out on a sunbed to read for hours and hours. Their dad was away a lot of time; he was a boss at Sun Life or some other big insurance company, and I knew nothing about his work except that his office was on the sixteenth floor of this huge skyscraper near the Cape Town foreshore.

The only part of their back garden that wasn't lawn, was near the fence, where there were beds of flowers and vegetables and fruit trees, including one loquat tree whose branches hung over our property.

My dad always said that possession is nine-tenths of the law (though at the time I didn't know what the heck he meant), and because of it we were entitled to take as many loquats from our side of the tree as we wanted. But we had to do it when Amos wasn't looking, because he had no regard for nine-tenths of the law, and when he once caught me pulling down a few loquats, he told me that if he ever caught me again stealing his loquats, he would tie me in the tree and let the birds eat me. I told my dad, and he said Amos didn't even know how to tie shoelaces, so how could he tie me in a tree. After that, I began to notice that Amos always wore his old pair of brown velskoen shoes with the shoelaces untied. You can tell a lot about a person just from the kind of shoes they wear and how they wear them.

Our servant girl Dolly never seemed to mind Amos's shoes. Often she would spend some of her day off chatting to him across the fence. The only time Amos ever looked anything less than angry was when Dolly spoke to him like that. I think he must've liked her company a lot, because he always stopped his weeding or whatever he was doing while he chatted to her.

Our house wasn't double storey and our backyard was a mess of weeds, but Hansel and Gretel liked it like that. They were our two tortoises – Hansel belonged to me and Gretel to my brother, Ivan – and they could hide in the weeds and make little burrows wherever they wanted without being told off by that Amos.

But sometimes I used to sit in the corner of my backyard, under the loquat tree, and look into the Neverland, which was my name for the Rudnik's back garden, watching Peter and Wendy and Ozzie riding their gleaming bikes or playing tennis in their white kits. If only I had been able to fly over the fence and over the loquat tree to play in that perfect weedless garden!

I used to think they must be the happiest kids in the world having a double-storey house and tennis court and swimming-pool, but even though I had such good feelings towards them, they never asked me or Ivan round to play. I suppose it's because we went to different schools.

I missed a lot of school myself because of sinus. And because of sinus I had to hang my head off the end of a bed over a bowl of steaming Friar's Balsam. After just a few minutes of this treatment, the mucus would loosen up, and I'd be forced to use a whole box of tissues. The amount of gunk that came out was truly phenomenal and made me seriously wonder what my body was made of.

I also have sinus to thank for the fact that at night my ma insisted I plug my nostrils with little cone-shaped wedges of raw carrot. This was something she read in her *Natural Remedies* book in the hope that it would improve my condition. It never did, though I must admit it often seemed to ease the pain for a while. The only permanent effect was that to this day whenever I see a carrot, I sneeze.

The best thing about sinus and staying home from school was the jigsaw puzzles. Ma always bought me a new jigsaw each time I was ill, so I had a huge collection. I used to like nothing better than to have a mixed-up box of a few hundred pieces, each with a different shape and colour, and watch them come together to make some sense of all the mess.

Although I missed so much school, my dad made up for it by teaching me a lot at home. He was a good teacher and I'm sure I learnt more from him than I would have by going to school.

One thing he taught me I'll never forget, and that was the power of nature.

This is how he taught it to me. He took me out in our backyard, and he had an ice-cube and a piece of wire and a lead weight. He stretched the wire across the top of the ice-cube and tied the weight to the wire, so that the wire was cutting into the ice.

Then he said we must leave the experiment for a few minutes. We went across to the loquat tree and pretended we were playing with Hansel and Gretel. But when Amos wasn't looking, we snitched a couple of loquats and ate them. As usual, I buried my loquat pip somewhere among the weeds in the hopes that it would grow into our own loquat tree one day. But none ever grew.

When we went back to the ice-cube, the wire was half way through. But it wasn't like cutting wood with a saw. Because as the wire made its way through the block, the ice above the wire refroze, so that you couldn't see where the wire had cut the cube. The wire was passing through the middle of the ice as if it had been pushed through like a needle and cotton.

'That's the power of nature,' my dad said, and I had to agree. 'It heals itself.'

I was glad to have that lesson by the time Aldred Nash and me played circus in our backyard.

That day Wendy was standing with her young brother Ozzie under the loquat tree and we asked them if they wanted to see a circus. Wendy was gorgeous, with freckles and pigtails, and spoke a very English English.

'I can go to the proper circus anytime I want to,' she said, 'and see real circus performers. So why ever should I want to watch you two?'

She was very stuck-up, Wendy was, but as she didn't walk off or anything, we reckoned she was keen on seeing a circus after all. Ozzie had a ringside seat, except that he had to peer at us through the diamond shapes of the wire fencing. On our side of the fence, there was an extra audience – Ivan sat on a fruit-box.

First Aldred tried to teach Hansel and Gretel to pull these little cardboard box carts, but when they wouldn't, he stood on their backs and said he was the tortoise rider at the circus. Ivan and me yelled at him to stop, because we knew Hansel and Gretel might get hurt, but he just continued.

'Go do your own tricks!' he said to me.

Ivan got wild; he's got a thing about animals. He ran inside to my ma screaming 'Aldred's killing Gretel! He's breaking her back!'

I got out this knife with a huge blade and said I was the swordfighter in the circus and that I'd cut Aldred in half if he didn't get off our pets.

'There aren't any swordfighters in a circus!' Aldred said, climbing off the tortoises.

'There are,' I said. 'In Boswell's circus.'

'Okay, then I'll be the swordfighter and you can be the liontamer.'

17

He tried to take the knife from me, but all he managed to get was the handle. I didn't want to be the liontamer, so I still held on to the blade. The only problem was when he pulled at it, the blade sliced my finger to the bone.

I didn't cry, at least not until I was out of sight of the loquat tree. And even then, my crying didn't last so long, because I remembered that nature had the power to heal my wound. The wound bled like mad which made me feel a bit wobbly in the knees, but I think Aldred was even more squeamish about blood than me, because he ran home immediately. Ma took me to the hospital where I had three stitches, and even now you can still see the scar where the skin healed over.

The next day Ivan and me went out into the backyard. We couldn't find Hansel and Gretel anywhere, but we did find a burrow at the edge of the lawn. I thought maybe they were hiding in there from sadists like Aldred. But perhaps it was already the beginning of winter and they were thinking of hibernating.

Ivan was upset. He got that way about animals. One time he came home from somewhere with this tiny black and white terrier following him.

'Who's dog's that?' my dad said.

'Mine,' Ivan said, untying the piece of rope around its neck.

'It's not.'

'It is,' Ivan pouted. 'It followed me home and possession is nine-tenths of the law, isn't it?'

The dog stayed about six weeks – sleeping in Ivan's room. He called it Titch. Personally, I thought it was an ugly little thing, but Ivan adored it. However, it disappeared as suddenly as it arrived. It probably followed some other little kid home and lived in his room for a few weeks. That's one way of surviving life as a dog.

But Ivan cracked up.

'I want Titch! I want him!'

He moaned and groaned for over a week, until no one could stand it any more. I think that's when we all started calling him Ivan the Terrible. In the end, he settled for a tortoise.

And now the tortoise had disappeared, Ivan was descending into one of his Terrible states. He had such bad feelings towards Aldred for standing on his pet.

'Let's send Aldred a peace-offering,' I suggested. 'Then you'll feel better.'

We bought a family-sized lemonade and rolled it in giftwrap, attaching a note saying 'To Aldred. You are my best friend. Here is some lemonade for you.' We left the bottle on his front stoep when no one was looking, hoping that he'd find it in due course. It goes without saying that we'd drunk the lemonade first and filled the bottle with a mixture of our urine and fizzy water.

I don't know if Aldred ever found out who the gift was from, but he never bothered to come round again, and Ivan's mood improved. Especially when my dad brought home a budgie for him.

That winter my sinus was bad. My ma bought me this huge puzzle of racing cars and my dad bought me a chart of the stars, which he said was educational, and a few comics, which were just for pleasure. Dr Ossip gave me six weeks of injections and at the end of it my backside felt like a sieve.

When the warm weather arrived, me and Ivan went to check if Hansel and Gretel had decided to emerge for summer.

But they hadn't. We then waited four years for them to come out, but they never did. And then we stopped waiting.

'Do you think they've escaped to the Never-neverland?' Ivan asked me.

'Maybe.'

By the time I was in my last year of Angelina Primary School, Ivan was in Sub A. My parents spoiled him terribly and because of that he had developed this nasty habit of always getting me into trouble with them.

We had invented this war game where we each sat on one side of the carpet, built castles out of Ivan's wooden bricks and then fired missiles at each other's defences. Of course, one time I missed Ivan's castle altogether and the wooden brick catapulted into the glass display cabinet. The glass hadn't even finished shattering before Ivan jumped up to tell on me. My ma told me it was my fault, because I was older, even though Ivan the Terrible had helped me to invent that game.

'Your dad's not going to be pleased,' she said.

At times like that I used to go out and stand under the loquat tree gazing across at Wendy and her mother. Wendy took after her mother, that's for sure; Mrs Rudnik was such a posh lady. The two of them used to sit on their patio and have afternoon drinks brought out to them by their house-boy. (Amos was only the garden boy.) I would watch Wendy and her mom laughing together.

When I got to high school I thought I would ask Wendy to come to the movies with me. It took a lot of planning. I had to decide whether to write her an invitation and pop it through her letterbox, or whether it would be better to call out to her one day when she was on the patio. I kept waiting for the right moment. And the longer I waited, the more she blossomed into a young Miss Rudnik, with refined manners and permed hair, and the more impossible it seemed that she would ever accept an invitation from anyone like me.

In the end, I waited too long.

One time I came home from school and found that a block of Upper Katzenellenbogen Street was completely sealed off by the police. It was the block with the Rudnik's house on it. There were several police cars and even one military vehicle parked at the end of the block.

When I got home I asked Dolly what the hell was going on.

'It's a bomb, Master,' she said to me. 'They found a bomb on the front stoep.'

'Who'd want to bomb the Rudniks, for God's sake?' I asked.

'I don't know,' Dolly said.

There had been a spate of bombs that year in police stations and shopping malls, but none as far as I knew, in private houses. Still, the nervousness was spreading that it would one day happen, and so many people in our area were learning to defend themselves at the new counter-terrorist schools.

Shortly after, there was a ring on our front doorbell. It was a policeman.

'We're asking everyone in the neighbourhood if they know anything about a giftwrapped parcel that's been left at the Rudnik residence,' he said.

'I don't know anything about it,' I said.

'Is there anyone else in this dwelling at the moment?'

'Just the maid, and my young brother Ivan.'

'Can you call them to the door, please.'

When Ivan came to the door and saw a policeman, he naturally got very shy. Dolly put her arms around him.

'Do either of you know anything about a giftwrapped ticking parcel that's been left at the Rudnik residence around the corner?'

Dolly shook her head, and Ivan hid behind her pink overall.

'Okay then, thank you,' the policeman said.

'Is there still any danger?' I asked.

'It's all under control, sir. The bomb disposal squad is handling the matter.'

The policeman continued his investigations next door.

About an hour later, there was a thudding explosion.

'God, it's gone off!'

Dolly and Ivan and me ran up to the corner of our street, only to discover that the ticking parcel had been removed by bomb experts to an open building plot nearby and deliberately blown up.

Later in the afternoon, the policeman knocked on our door again, asking if anyone recognized this burnt out fragment of a Mickey Mouse clock.

This time Ivan couldn't deny it, because I was standing there and it was my birthday present to him just a few months before.

'Do you know what trouble you've caused?' the policeman asked him.

'He's just a child,' Dolly said, hugging him close. 'He didn't know it was trouble. He wanted to give his clock to the little boy there. He just want to be friends. He's a innocent child.'

'Where's your parents?' the policeman asked me, ignoring Dolly's apology on behalf of Ivan.

'They're working. They'll be back later.'

'Ja, well, they'll get the full report from us.'

When I got to school next day, everyone was talking about the terrorist bomb that had gone off in our neighbourhood.

'It was a bigger bomb than the one at Eastville police station,' Stuart Spiro said.

'It was Cuban designed,' Chris Tomsett said. I didn't bother to tell him that the Mickey Mouse clock was made in Hong Kong.

The bomb incident reduced my chances of going out with Wendy to a virtual zero. I imagined she wasn't too pleased with our family for the bother we had caused.

But the virtual zero became an actual zero a few months later.

I was playing table tennis with my dad in the front room while my ma was reading the paper, when she suddenly cried out 'Oh my God!'. My Dad said 'What's wrong?' and went over and put his arm tenderly around her. She couldn't speak; she just pointed to the newspaper. It was the death-notices, I could tell. My ma always read the personal columns, the births, weddings and deaths.

My ma cried and my dad poured himself a brandy, which was very unusual if he didn't have guests.

'What's wrong?' I asked. 'What's happened?'

'It's Mrs Rudnik,' my dad said. 'She's dead.'

The next time I saw Peter and Wendy and Ozzie, I was in the backyard and they were on the patio with lots of visitors, most of them in black dresses and suits. Amos was keeping out of the way, sitting in his room. Just once I saw him, standing at the door of his room, looking at the congregation of white people, and shaking his head slowly from side to side.

All those people looked like different pieces of jigsaw puzzle scrambled up in a box, but there was no way of making the scene come together because one of the most important pieces was missing. Wendy was looking so pretty, wearing a dark blue outfit, but I went indoors before she could see me staring at her.

After that one time, I never saw any of the Rudniks again, until I saw Wendy that day in the Spur.

The new owners of the house were quite brave. I thought they must be to live in a house where the lady threw herself from the sixteenth storey of a skyscraper in the middle of Cape Town. I've never managed to eat another loquat from that tree since Mrs Rudnik's suicide.

As I stood at the counter paying for my coffee, thinking back on Peter and Wendy and Ozzie, I still remembered what my dad said about the power of nature, and how I always hoped for their sakes it was true, because their wound was bigger than the scar on my finger.

I could see that scar clearly as I held the coffee in my hand and I thought, should I go join Wendy or would it bring back too painful memories for her?

'Come on!' I said to myself. 'Go and say hello! At least see if she's friendly.'

I turned to walk over to her table, but she and her friend had gone and all that was left were half-empty coffee cups.

Ladybug

'Get out of the sun, woman,' my dad would say to my ma, after a spell of sunbathing. 'You're beginning to look like a shochadicke.'

Of course, just how dark you have to be to count as a black person was a mystery to me. I'll give you a for instance: at Muizenberg beach you'd see whites of all different colours – I mean skins ranging from the sickly white colour of an upturned frog to that of a dark Albany bitter chocolate passing through a pink, speckled boerewors colour and even sometimes a painful tomato red, when a fair person caught too much of the midday sun.

It was easier to check out the naturalness of those colours on girls and women, because often they would lie there with their bikini straps undone. That was the time to walk round and make a tour of inspection to see if their skin was whiter on the bits of breast that was showing now that the straps were loosened.

To me, my ma just looked suntanned, but I must admit there were coloureds who had much lighter skin than her.

My ma has always loved sunbathing. Especially on the weekends. She lays out on this canvas bed on our stoep for hours and hours, and even my dad's comments about her beginning to look like a non-white had no effect on her. She worships the sun, I think.

My best friend, Dewie, and me used to often argue about

whether Hester Conradie was a coloured or not. She lived in our road, but not on the same side as us. On our side the houses were all quite new, and definitely, without the shadow of a doubt, all the occupants were white, even if some of their husbands made comments about how dark their tan was getting.

But the opposite side of the road was a completely different ballgame. There were just three shabby houses there, and one of them was hidden behind this huge hedge. I'm not kidding, this hedge grew taller than a lamppost.

It was a good hedge because it had these sort of bluebell creepers entwined in it with their leaves all eaten into patterns by the ladybugs. Sometimes I used to catch a ladybug in a jar, drop a few vineleaves in for her to eat, and then keep it in my room for a few days. I liked those ladybugs because they were bright yellow with black marks, (or were they black with yellow marks?).

You couldn't see any of the Conradie's house from our road because of the hedge, but if you looked up their gravel drive, you could see an old dilapidated tin-roofed house.

Our deliberations about Hester were very vague, mostly for the reason that we didn't see much of her. I mean she was always wearing dresses and a jersey, so it wasn't that easy to tell what colour she was.

'She's as dark as Caroline,' Dewie would say. Caroline was the coloured servant in his house.

'But not as dark as Dolly,' I would reply. Dolly was our servant, and was half coloured, half black.

Hester wasn't there that much. I think she lived part of the time with some family outside Cape Town. We only used to see her during school holidays, and that was only after we learnt about climbing the hedge.

That was a long time ago when we were pikkies. We found this hole into the hedge, and then you could climb up the main trunk of the bush until you had popped out above the leaves, level with the top of the lamppost.

We were able to make a den up there, a sort of crow's-nest hollowed out of the leaves and branches, and it was large enough for us both to lie down in – no trouble.

Often during holidays, we would sneak into our hole and climb up to the den with a picnic lunch. From there we could look down on people waiting at the bus-stop and we could watch the cars going up Bishopston Drive. But best of all we could see into the Conradie's yard, and we even had a good view of their tin-roofed house.

If my dad had known we were up there, he would have killed us, for sure. And if Dewie's dad had known we were up there, he would have done even worse than kill us. Because my dad thought the Conradies were poor whites and also a bit mad in the head. Dewie's dad, on the other hand, reckoned the Conradies were coloureds who were a bit mad in the head.

At least they were both agreed that the Conradies were a bit mad in the head. That's because they both believed that Mr Conradie didn't do any work, and Mrs Conradie started howling every full moon.

From our crow's-nest in the hedge, I must admit we never saw Mr Conradie do much work, but his vegetable garden always looked in good shape to us although we didn't personally see him digging there very often. But we never saw Mrs Conradie howl at the full moon. Mind you, we never saw the full moon shining in broad daylight either. It was something we used to consider in our braver moments: whether to wake up one midnight and climb into the hedge to watch Mrs Conradie howling at the full moon.

'I bet she lifts her head up towards the moon like a wolf,' Dewie said.

'You've never seen a wolf howling at the moon!' I said.

But if we didn't see all that much of the parents, we were often fortunate enough to catch sight of Hester swinging on this rope that hung from a branch of her eucalyptus or riding her broken two wheeler round the garden. Sometimes she saw us up there in our hedge, but she never told on us and we just used to wave to her, and sometimes she waved back.

I guess we would have gone on arguing about Hester Conradie's colour even when we became teenagers if it wasn't for bumping into Eric Kritzinger during one school holiday.

'Have you been to take a look at Hester Conradie?' he asked Dewie and me.

'No, why should we?' we asked.

'Haven't you heard then?' he said.

'Heard what?'

'That she's showing herself to the boys for money.'

'You're kidding us, man, aren't you?'

'No way. I've been to see her.'

'Hell man, what did you see?' I asked him.

'Everything. I gave her one rand. Twenty-five cents to see her tits, twenty-five cents to see the rest of her, twenty-five cents to feel her one tit, and twenty-five cents for the other.'

'Hell man, how do we get to see her?'

'Round the block you'll see this hole in the big hedge, and you'll see the queue of boys waiting to go in.'

Dewie and me didn't waste much time, except to go into our houses and get money from our rooms.

Then down the road and around the block.

True enough, there were three boys queuing, and we stood behind them. One of the boys was Rael Chandler but I'd never laid eyes on either of the other two before. From the look of them, the news about Hester's business must have already reached Oudtshoorn. Rael winked at us as we queued up at the end of the line.

'Have you touched a girl before in those places?' I whispered to Dewie.

'Stacks of times, man. Haven't you?'

'Of course, I was just wondering about you,' I said.

After a while, a boy came out from the hole in the hedge. It was Henry van Breda. He came out licking his lips and rolling his eyes. Then he wolfwhistled and made gestures with his hands like she had big ones and he'd had a good time.

The next boy went through the hole.

I never knew there was a hole around that part of the hedge. Mind you, it had been years since I had climbed up into the crow's-nest.

Another boy I'd never seen before joined the queue behind us, and this drip of a boy, Rodney Hershel, also showed up.

'What's going on?' he asked.

'Don't you know?' Dewie said. Dewie couldn't stand Rodney, for some reason.

'But is she really letting boys see her?' Rodney asked.

'Why don't you join the queue and find out?'

'I would, honestly,' Rodney said. 'But I'm on my way to see the doctor. My adenoids are bad. Maybe another time I can.'

'Your adenoids are always bad,' Dewie said. 'By the time your adenoids let you join the queue, Hester will be an old granny.'

Rodney skulked off.

'He's such a nebbish,' Dewie said to me.

After a short while it was Rael's turn. He was dressed really flashy for the occasion, or was it that he was always a flash dresser? He was ever ready to impress girls. He winked at us as he went in and he winked at us again as he came out five minutes later.

Only one boy to go, I thought, as I felt tremors of excitement and nervousness eating at my pants.

'Now we'll see if she's white or coloured,' Dewie said to me. 'You must check her hair. If it's in korreltjies and feels all wiry then she's coloured. And if she hasn't got moons on her fingernails that also means she's a coloured. And you must check whether the colour of her tits is different to the rest of her. If it's not then she's a coloured for sure.'

The boy before us came out with his cheeks looking a painful tomato red, as if he'd been stupid enough to bathe in the midday sun. He must have been the sort of boy who embarrassed easily. I hoped I wouldn't come out with my embarrassment lit up like a neon light for the whole of Claremont to see.

Dewie looked at me and said 'Who first?'

We did ching, ching, cha, and Dewie won because stone is stronger than scissors.

He disappeared through the hole. I stood by the hedge and watched a yellow and black ladybug nibbling away at the leaf of that bluebell creeper.

After a few minutes Dewie emerged.

'Is she white or coloured?' I asked him.

'Go see for yourself!'

I crawled through the hole and found Hester waiting with her finger near her mouth saying 'Shh!' She obviously wanted me to be quiet so that her father wouldn't discover that she was using his shed. And what's more, she wasn't using it for horticultural purposes either.

The shed was conveniently situated quite near to the hedge and she led me in immediately.

'Hi!' she said, shutting the door behind us. 'How much money have you brought?'

It was quite dark in that shed, because the only window had a sheet of black plastic nailed over it. But even in that semidarkness, illuminated only by chinks of light trickling around the edges of the plastic, I could see that she had changed a lot since we used to spy down on her from our crow's-nest. Boy, had she changed! I wondered if I should tell her I'd forgotten my money, and that I'd come back the next day instead.

'Here's a rand.'

'Good,' she said.

She took off her jersey and stood there with her breasts exposed. They were the loveliest things I had ever seen.

'Okay?' she said.

'Ja, okay,' I said.

Then she let her jersey fall back down to her waist and she dropped her skirt to the floor and pulled down her pants for a second.

It felt funny to me, looking at her private triangle of hair.

'Okay?' she said.

'Ja, okay,' I said.

She pulled her pants back on and fastened her skirt and then she moved towards the door.

'I paid a rand,' I said.

'So you got everything for a rand. What more do you expect?'

'Don't I get to feel your . . .'

'That stupid Eric Kritzinger. He tells everyone a load of trash. I wouldn't let anyone touch me. Do you think I'm cheap or something?'

'No, I don't,' I said. 'I'm sorry.'

She led me back through the hole and I said goodbye and thanks.

'Well, is she white or coloured?' Dewie asked.

Jeez, I had forgotten to notice.

'What do you think?' I asked.

'Coloured,' he said. 'What do you think?'

'White,' I said.

'Wasn't it good feeling her tits?' Dewie said.

'Ja,' I said, wondering if she had let him touch her but not me.

'But I think she must be a bit mad, like her mom and dad, to let boys do that,' Dewie said.

I could have told Dewie that I had once quite long ago doubledared his own sister Nolene to undress and stand in front of her bedroom window while I counted to ten. And she did it, and even let me count to fifty, and what's more she didn't charge me a rand either. Mind you, she was so skinny at the time, she couldn't really have charged too much anyway. But I didn't want Dewie to think his own sister was mad, so I didn't tell him.

The next day I was up early and I went round the block to the hole in the hedge. I had another rand's worth of pocket money because I thought I'd just go back and check if Hester was really coloured or white.

But as I turned the corner, I saw that Dewie was already queuing. Obviously he also wanted to recheck Hester to see what colour she was. I waited half an hour until I saw Dewie go back to his own house. Then I went to do my checking.

I gave her my rand and she showed me everything again, but still I wasn't sure at all if she was coloured or white.

'Why do you do this?' I asked her.

'For pocket money,' she said.

'It's a good way to make pocket money,' I said.

'Ja,' she said.

'Can I come again tomorrow?' I asked.

'It's your money,' she said.

It's true I was running out of money, so I offered to clean my dad's car, and when that was finished I cleaned Mr Aubrey's car down the road, and then Mrs Gross's car, but I couldn't clean Mr Swimmer's car because he said Dewie had already done it.

On my fourth visit I still hadn't made up my mind about Hester, but I asked her if she would like to come the next day with me to help me clean cars to earn more pocket money for herself.

She said thanks for the offer, but she was off to her new boarding school the next day.

I was sorry she was leaving and I told her so. But although she went away, she left behind many images that remained in our heads for months, if not years. In fact, those sort of images are painted in waterproof colours. They don't wash out and will probably last as long as our heads last.

After I said goodbye to her, Dewie and me had a discussion and we figured that Hester must after all be white to go to that boarding school.

'So I was right all along,' I said, wanting the last word.

But the day she was due to go, Dewie changed his mind again when we saw a boy queuing at the hole in the hedge and he was as dark as a bitter Albany chocolate.

'No white girl would show herself to a non-white, would she?' Dewie argued. 'So I was right all along.'

'But isn't that boy Tony Daniels from Wynberg Boys?' I asked.

So then the deliberations had to start all over again about whether Tony now was coloured or white.

The one that got away

'This bladdy ocean is empty, I'm sure of it.'

That's what Rael said to me after we had been fishing on these boulders near Seaforth for about five hours. From that comment you can easily see that he was the sort of person who quickly jumped to conclusions. And not always the right conclusions, either.

'They're just not biting today,' I said.

'Well you wait for them to bite, okay? – while I go check out some of the action on that beach.'

From the fact that he deserted me, you can probably deduce that Rael didn't have the patience of a true fisherman. He only accompanied me out of friendship.

In the distance I could see him chatting up some girls. And even from where I was sitting I could tell they were wearing skimpy bikinis. Rael was the sort of person who judges a girl's personality by her bikini: the less bikini, the more personality.

Well, there I am, with my fisherman's patience, still waiting for a bite, when this person approaches me, and I can tell you, this person wasn't wearing a bikini, and he wouldn't have looked good in one either. He wore a suit, even in the midday heat, and not only a suit, but a priest's collar around his neck. Just my luck, I thought, to be pestered by a priest, when I could have gone with Rael to chat up those girls in their skimpy bikinis.

34

'Those fish are crafty devils, hey!' this priest says to me.

Here he goes, I thought. First, he starts with the devil, then he'll tell me about my sins . . .

'As soon as one of those fish sees the bait at the end of your line, he sends a warning telegram to all his relations.'

The priest had no sooner said this than I got this heavy tug on my line.

'You've got one there, my boy!'

As I reeled in the line, my rod doubled over in an arch. The priest fellow was getting himself all worked up.

'Reel him in! You've got a whopper!'

I yanked and tugged, thinking Rael would kick himself for going off just when the fish started biting.

The priest was almost down on his hands and knees. For a moment I thought he was praying, but he was just trying to get a glimpse of my catch as it got nearer to the surface.

My reel was almost full when the line went as limp as a wet handshake. It emerged from the water with the bait missing. Also, the hook and the sinker!

'That must have been one hungry fish,' the priest said.

As I attached a new hook, he notices Rael's fishing rod lying there.

'Is that rod being used?' he asks me.

'I can't see anyone using it,' I said.

'I meant, do you think . . . I mean, could I have a go?'

'It's my friend's rod, but he won't mind if you use it.'

'Great!' the priest said, picking up the rod. 'I used to fish a lot in the old days, until someone came along and asked me to be a fisher of men.'

Here comes the propaganda, I thought. Now I'll hear all about how Jesus came into his heart and told him to go fishing for men.

'This is the life!' the priest said, taking off his jacket and rolling up his sleeves. 'Hot sun, blue sky, sea and salt air, and a rod in his hands. What more could a man want, hey?'

It probably would have ruined his fun if he knew that he

was sitting next to a person of Jewish blood. So I didn't breathe a word.

But he sure knew how to get me talking.

'When did you learn to fish?' he asked.

I told him that about nine years ago, me and my dad used to go fishing a lot at Cape Town docks; in fact, it was nearly every weekend.

We used to first drop off Ma and my young brother, Ivan, at my grandparents' house in Salt River. It was a huge old house with a big backyard where my grandfather kept his chickens. Then on the way back from the docks, we'd stop at the house for a meal, pick up my ma and Ivan and show them what we'd caught – usually nothing.

'Just like today,' the priest said, 'the rascals won't bite.'

Anyways, before long, he's got me talking about my grandparents' house in Salt River and I'm telling him how I used to sneak upstairs to have a look at Mr Coetzee.

I didn't know if I was boring the priest or not, so I waited a moment.

'Who's this Mr Coetzee?' he asked.

So I told him that Mr Coetzee was a skeleton in my Uncle Arthur's room. It was standing there behind the door like it was also waiting to be called down for an evening meal. I didn't like to touch those bleached bones, held together with bits of wire, but I couldn't help going to say hello to it each time I was in that house. One thing I'll never forget about Mr Coetzee – his skull was sawn in half horizontally, and it was hinged at the back, so you could lift the lid to see inside. It was as hollow as an empty ostrich egg.

'What was a skeleton doing in that house?' the priest asked me.

I explained that my Uncle Arthur was a medical student at that time, (he's qualified now), and the skeleton was being stored in his room for some reason – maybe for study purposes.

The priest seemed really interested in what I had to say, so I talked and it whiled away the afternoon.

I told him that sometimes Uncle Arthur used to joke with me.

'Hey, Baz,' he would say to me. 'You know why Mr Coetzee's bones are so white?'

I never knew, so I couldn't answer.

'Because he was a white man when he was alive.'

'You're kidding me, Uncle Arthur, aren't you?'

He never answered me, and for a while I really wondered about the colour of those old bones. Of course, I was only about eight-years-old then.

My grandfather's butchery was three blocks away from the house and sometimes my dad used to drop me off there to walk home with my grandfather. There were carcasses everywhere, hanging on these coathooks in long rows, dripping blood on to the fresh clean sawdust that Kosie used to sprinkle on to the concrete floor.

Kosie and my grandfather both used to wear these bloodstained aprons, but only my grandfather used to cut the meat in front of the customers, unless the customer was also coloured like Kosie.

Usually the meals we ate at my grandparents' house were chicken – probably one that had been squawking around the backyard earlier that afternoon. Sometimes, Kosie used to let me help him catch the chickens for my grandfather to slaughter in the kosher way . . .

I stopped talking. I suddenly felt embarrassed, because I had let the kosher bit slip out without noticing it. Now the priest would surely realize he was sitting next to a Jewish person, and that might spoil his afternoon.

'Go on,' he said to me. 'Tell me about the kosher slaughtering.'

So I told him that my grandfather used to slit the chicken's neck. Kosie used to make a game of catching those chickens with me. We used to run around the yard flapping our arms, saying 'Kom chickie-chick! Kom na Kosie!'

'I can just picture it,' the priest said.

So I told him more about Kosie who had no teeth in his mouth at all, but the biggest smile in Cape Town.

I remember the time my dad became manager of Rosco Furnishings he bought an almost-new Chevrolet. It was so almost-new that even the upholstery still had that nice leather-polish smell. The next time we stopped at my grandparents' house to drop off my ma and Ivan, the whole family came out to look at it. My dad gave everyone a ride in it, except Kosie, who was smiling so much at the new car he didn't want to move from the pavement. We drove around a few blocks and when we returned there was Kosie's smile, still on the pavement like a Cheshire cat.

The priest reeled in his line, checked the bait and cast out again.

'So you were telling me about your grandparents,' he said, and the way he said it made me wonder whether he was fishing more in that sea or more in my memory. Still, as I said, it was better than fisherman's patience for passing time, so I continued.

I told him that at the time of that drive in the new car, my grandmother had two legs. My grandfather used to love both of her legs, even though she had to inject her thighs with insulin every morning because of her diabetes. Anyhow, in the old days, long before, they used to go dancing together at this place called the Blue Moon, and in their house they had lots of dance music. My grandmother was mad on Frank Sinatra and often they would dance around their lounge to show Ivan and me how it used to be at the Blue Moon.

I don't think Ivan liked their performances much, because one day he put a Frank Sinatra record in the middle of the room and stood on it. My grandmother was upset – but my grandfather spoiled us terribly. He got down the whole pile of Frank Sinatra's records and made stepping stones for Ivan all around the room.

'Let him have fun, Bobba!' he said to my granny. 'You're only young once!'

My grandmother was not too pleased. She stared daggers at my grandfather and said to him in Yiddish: 'May you stay healthy, but why do you allow him to do that?' Then she walked out of the room in protest.

Unfortunately at the end of that year she got a bad thrombosis in her right leg and the gangrene set in, so she had to have it amputated above the right knee. After that, she didn't dance to those Frank Sinatra records any more . . .

Again my talking came to a stop. Perhaps I shouldn't be talking about my grandmother's leg to a stranger, even if he was a priest. If my ma ever found out, she'd go mad.

'Is it painful to remember?' the priest asked me. 'You don't have to talk about it if you don't want.'

I told him that it was my ma, really, who found it so depressing. She took it very badly.

'Such a zest for life Bobba always had,' is about all my ma could say about it. 'Do you remember how she used to love the sea? She used to stand in the waves and scoop the water over her body with one hand . . .'

Then my ma would bite some of the skin around her wrist to stop herself bursting into tears.

'Such a zest for life, and now she's a . . .'

The word always stuck in her mouth, but what she meant was 'cripple'.

'Are your grandparents still alive?' the priest asked.

I told him they were. Soon after the operation they sold their house in Salt River and bought a small flat in Sea Point. Later they sold that as well, and moved into an old age home.

Sometimes, when I visit them, I find my grandfather watching my grandmother strapping the artificial leg to her thigh-stump, or injecting the insulin into that stump. I must admit it's always made me feel faint: it is partly the smell of ether, partly the sight of the stump itself. But it must pain my grandfather more. I always see tears in his eyes – such tears that make a person realize how much he used to love both of her legs.

'Life is a fragile and mysterious thing,' the priest said, looking straight at me. 'You never know how it's going to turn out, do you?'

I thought, watch out, here it comes – how I better turn to Jesus for help and comfort and salvation and all the other fringe benefits.

But the priest just looked down into the ocean for a while. In the distance I could see Rael frolicking with the two skimpy girls in the waves. They were ducking each other and laughing.

'What was it like fishing at Cape Town docks?' the priest asked me. 'I've never fished there. Did you have more luck than here?'

I told him our luck was the same all round the Cape, but me and my dad used to have good times there. Then I decided to tell him about this one time before my grandmother's operation when my dad dropped my ma and Ivan off at the house in Salt River, and we drove on to the docks as usual. It was a hot morning and the docks were mostly asleep – no big ships going in and out of the harbour. My dad fished along the breakwater that day, as usual, and there were about a hundred other fishermen stretched out in a long line. (Maybe that's an exaggeration, but there were a lot.) I think they were more skilled than my dad, because they used sharp iron gaffs to pull out snoek and all these other huge fish they managed to catch.

Mostly my dad used to catch seaweed, which tugged the hardest on his line and often broke it, or blaasops, which are poisonous and puff themselves up into a bag of air . . .

'Ja, those I've caught many of in my time,' the priest said.

. . . or octopus, which you have to throw back into the sea with the hook still in its mouth, but occasionally my dad caught a small red roman – and then my ma would be pleased when we came home, because there'd be something at least to show for a whole day's outing.

'Come on, you bliksem red romans!' the priest shouted towards the sea. 'Come have a little nibble!'

The priest bobbed his line up and down, then said: 'Oh sorry, please continue!'

In those days I never used to fish, I told him. Well, I did – for about a half an hour until I got bored. But then I'd get fed up with waiting for nothing to happen, and I used to wander off to get away from the smell of buckets of bait and dying fish. Mostly I climbed these huge stacks of rusty iron girders or I climbed this sort of small lighthouse and looked down on the row of fishermen.

But on this one particular day I had to come down unexpectedly from the lighthouse because the fisherman next to my dad caught something on his hook that wasn't seaweed or a blaasop or an octopus or a red roman or a snoek. It was a coloured.

'How do you mean he caught a coloured?' the priest asked.

I explained that this coloured had walked behind the fisherman just as he was casting his line, and the hook caught in his neck with the full force of the fisherman's thrust.

'Oh, Jesus!' the priest said, screwing up his face agonizingly. (That was the first mention of his religion the whole afternoon.)

The hook was buried in the coloured's flesh, I told the priest, maybe even in his throat, and the lead sinker was dangling like a useless bell on a cow.

'Ag, why don't you look where you walk?' the fisherman said.

'Sorry, meneer,' the coloured said, though his speech

was raspy and hampered by the damage to his throat. 'I didn't see you throwing your line.'

'Next time, open your eyes man, or you'll get killed.'

'Ja, meneer.'

The priest shook his head from side to side, making little sucking sounds: 'Tch, tch, tch. Some people, hey, think the world owes them a living.'

I went on describing the incident, how the fisherman produced rusty old scissors and cut off the line and sinker.

'Now let's get that hook out,' the fisherman said.

He searched through his fishing box until he found a strong pair of wire-cutters.

'The best thing to do,' he said, 'is to push the barb all the way through, until it comes out of the skin, then snip off the barb and pull out the rest of the hook.'

The coloured was not keen, especially as the fisherman was the size of a Western Province prop-forward and looked much more like a welder than a surgeon. His huge white hands were rough and calloused, as if accustomed to holding red-hot metals.

'Please, no, meneer, it will hurt, it's too sore, ag, please, no, meneer!'

'Just be still!' the welder said. 'It will only hurt once.'

But the coloured slipped out of his grasp like a wet fish.

'Surely it needs a doctor,' my dad said. 'Otherwise it could get infected. These hooks are not so clean.'

This time the priest nodded his head, perhaps seeing my father's good intentions.

I told him that the welder was indignant about my dad butting in.

'What do you know about my hooks?' the welder asked my dad.

'It's not just *your* hooks. Shouldn't you take him to a hospital?' my dad said.

'Well, I'm not spoiling my day's fishing for someone so stupid to get himself hooked like that. You can take him to

42

the coloured hospital if you want,' the welder said, settling down again to attend his fishing rod.

'Alright,' my dad said, 'I'll take him.'

The welder spat on the concrete beside him, his bull-neck puffing out over his jersey, to indicate his contempt for my dad's interference.

'That hook could be out already if I would have snipped it,' the welder said.

My dad packed up his fishing gear without giving the welder a glance, but as we walked back down the break-water past the line of fishermen, my dad couldn't help moaning with regret because so many of them were catching snoek left, right and centre.

'What a waste, Bazzie,' my dad said to me. 'Those snoek are just asking to be caught today.'

'Sorry, meneer,' the coloured said.

He sat quietly in the back of the car, with the hook still in his neck. I remember turning around to examine the wound, just in case I could make out what colour his bones were, but there was so much blood pouring out, I decided to open the window instead – it wasn't that I was feeling faint or anything, but the coloured's vinegary smell didn't go well with almost-new leather polish, and anyway, blood has a strange effect on some people's stomachs. My dad passed the windscreen-cloth to the coloured to mop up the blood leaking from his wound.

'What the hell were you doing on the breakwater anyway?' my dad asked. 'You weren't going to fish there, were you?'

'No, I was just sommer strolling.'

My dad stopped at the hospital and helped the man out of the car. He went inside with the coloured and signed him into the accidents department.

'Will you be okay now?' my dad asked him.

'Ja, dankie, meneer! Best wishes, meneer!'

On the way back I remember my dad saying: 'Imagine

walking so close to someone casting a line. You've got to be stupid to do something like that, hey?'

The priest considered my dad's words. 'Well, I suppose it isn't the most sensible thing to do,' he said. 'But still, your father helped the coloured man and that was a very Christian thing to do.'

I stared right into the priest's eyes, wondering how he could dare say that to me. Probably next thing he'd be giving me a Bible.

'Oh, sorry, I meant that was a very Jewish thing to do. No, no! I didn't mean that either. I meant it was a very human thing to do. Ja, that's what I meant.'

I agreed with the priest and told him that after going to the coloured hospital, we picked my ma and Ivan up from my grandparents' house, and my ma was disappointed as usual because we didn't catch any fish to eat. But Ivan found red splodges of blood on the almost-new car seats, and so my dad said that he had caught a red roman, and that we had put it on the back seat, but then it got away.

The afternoon had passed quickly with all the talking and I wasn't surprised when Rael suddenly returned. But I didn't expect him to have the two skimpy girls with him.

'Hey, Baz! This is Lee-Anne and this is Charmian. She wants to meet you.'

The girls were dressed only in their skimpy bikinis and I could immediately see that both girls had lots of personality. I only hoped that my friend the priest appreciated that much personality as well.

'Hey, who said you could use my rod?' Rael said cheekily to the priest. Of course, he couldn't have known it was a priest straight off, because the collar wasn't that visible from behind.

'It was me,' I explained to Rael. 'I said you wouldn't mind.'

'Anyway,' the priest said, 'I must be going now, so you can have the rod back.'

He handed it over to Rael and I could see Rael felt bad about accusing a priest.

'Thanks for the loan of it,' the priest said. 'I've had a marvellous afternoon.'

He rolled down his sleeves, put on his jacket and held out his arm to shake my hand.

'Thanks very much for your company. I've enjoyed talking to you and hearing about your life and about that welder who was a fisher of men.'

We said our goodbyes.

'Excuse me, ladies,' the priest said, as he walked away across the rocks.

'Hells-teeth, Basil,' Rael said, 'have you been converted here today or what?'

Which goes to prove, yet again, that Rael was the sort of person who quickly jumped to conclusions.

History lesson

Have you noticed how in life one thing always leads to another?

It's taken me all the eighteen years of my life to work that one out, but now I'm sure of it: one thing definitely always leads to another. I mean, if it didn't, how would we ever get anywhere?

The only difficulty is working out which thing led to which other thing. Usually you can only find out afterwards, but it would be a great help to know in advance, wouldn't it? The person who figures that out will definitely win a Nobel Prize, I reckon. Maybe it will be me, one day, who knows?

Take the business that happened during that one history lesson in my second last year at high school. Now there's a fascinating case of how one thing led to another.

You see, the trouble was that Lewis had this degenerating disease. He looked half spastic and had to stop every few moments to suck in his spit and gasp for breath. But he was okay as a teacher. At least he tried to bring history to life by pretending the class was the eastern frontier of the Cape and dividing us into whites and Xhosas.

But one morning it wasn't Lewis that walked into the classroom for history. It was Tobias, the headmaster, with this piece of hotstuff next to him.

'Unfortunately Mr Lewis won't be with us any more,'

Tobias said, but I didn't catch any of the details. I was too busy looking at the lady. She looked like this goddess that had just walked straight out of Hollywood with stacks of make-up, high-heeled shoes, long red fingernails, and a spectacular shape of a body. I can tell you without a shadow of exaggeration that I wasn't the only boy in that class who didn't hear what exactly had happened to poor old Lewis. All our eyes were focused on one point, or maybe I should rather say two points.

'Miss Shales will be taking over from Mr Lewis,' Tobias explained, and a few of the boys couldn't hide the smiles that the comparison between Lewis's broken body and the spectacular shape of the new teacher brought to their faces.

'I hope you'll make her feel very welcome and will give her the same kind of co-operation you gave Mr Lewis – perhaps a bit more.'

Looking round the class at that moment, you couldn't have helped noticing that all the boys were deep in thought about ways to welcome her.

'I'll leave you now in her capable hands,' Tobias said, and he slipped out the door.

I stared at Miss Shales's capable hands: soft and delicate and with those pointy polished red fingernails.

I stared at her capable legs: beautifully shaped and stockinged, fitting neatly into her high-heeled shoes.

I stared at her capable face: lipsticked lips, eye-shadowed eyes, pert nose, flushed cheeks.

And I also stared at her capable breasts . . .

'What's your name?' Miss Shales asked, pointing directly at me.

'Who, Miss?' I asked.

'The one who's staring. You!'

'Basil Kushekushenovitz.'

The class burst out laughing.

'Don't be funny, boy. I asked for your name, not your warcry.'

'It's Basil Kushekushekushenovitz, Miss.'

I had never stammered with my name before, but suddenly it seemed like the hardest word in the world to get out of my mouth, especially with Miss Cape Town herself parading in front of you and thirty-six other boys laughing their heads off.

'Alright then, that's enough of your name. I expect I'll get used to it. Let's get on with some history.'

Who knows what we studied that day, because I don't remember a word of it. Nor the next few lessons either. All I remember is that it was harder for me to breathe during history than it used to be. And I don't think it was because we got on to the topic of the discovery of diamonds in Kimberley.

It was in the third lesson that my troubles really got worse. They started because of this boy Eric Kritzinger who was older than me and stupider than me. In fact he was stupider than all the boys in the class – that's what everyone said afterwards.

He always sat in the back row of the classroom where he could get on famously with doing nothing. But just before this one history lesson, I noticed that everyone had turned around to see what Eric was up to. I also turned around and couldn't believe my eyes. The stupid boy had opened his fly and was holding his own thing in his hand. It was all below desk level; all you could see above was this idiotic smile on Eric's face.

Miss Shales came in and started her history lesson, talking about Griquas and the British and the rush for diamonds. While she was reading us this one section from the text book, a voice shouted out 'Your stocking is laddered, Glinda!'

I didn't realize a laddered stocking could cause that much bother, but Miss Shales jumped up and asked 'Who said that?'

She looked around the class at every single boy and then she found the smile on Eric's face.

'Wipe that smile off your face immediately, Eric, and come here!'

I could see Eric's hands under the desk furiously trying to pack away certain parts of his anatomy, while the top half of him was playing for time.

'Yes, Miss, I've just got pins and needles in my leg, Miss.'

Eventually he stood up and walked to the front of the class. He stood before Miss Shales with his fly half done up and a bit of white shirt sticking out.

'How dare you call me by my first name?' she yelled at him as she stood up from her seat by the table. It was then that I could see her ladder to paradise. It started somewhere at her calf and passed up beyond her knee, over her thigh, then disappeared into Griqualand West.

'Sorry, Miss,' Eric said.

Miss Shales cast a fiery look at him.

'I don't know how you found out my first name, but I assure you its use is reserved for my close acquaintances and you are not one of them and never will be. You do not have the right, nor my permission to ever again use my first name. Is that understood?'

'Yes, Miss.'

'Go back to your seat.'

'Yes,' Eric said, turning to go back to his seat. 'It's okay with me, Glinda,' he added, under his breath, and some more laughter broke out in that class.

'What did you say?'

'Nothing, Miss.'

That Eric was so cocksure of himself. Either that or he was suffering from a severe shortage in the brains department.

Later in the same lesson, Glinda asked me to read from the text book. It was just this bit about the Big Hole at

Kimberley, but as I started to read I began to feel very wobbly.

'Are you alright, Kushykush?' Glinda said.

I felt much worse when she came and stood over me and her perfume drifted up my nostrils and into my lungs like smoke from a delirious fire. I could see her from the toes in her high-heel shoes upwards to about the level of her neck. But I didn't want to lift my eyes to look into her face.

'Are you alright?' she asked again. 'You look pale.'

She was wearing a short orange skirt with flowers and a little tightfitting jersey. And her ladder was still waiting to be climbed.

'Okay, read for us now, Basil. We're all waiting.'

I took a deep breath and started to read about the biggest man-made hole in the world, but I could feel something rattling in my throat – a ball or a lump of something, like those pellets of undigested skin and bones which get regurgitated by owls – and no voice emerged from my throat. My lips were moving and I had the feeling I was reading aloud, but my voice had other ideas; it was taking a short holiday to Oudtshoorn. As the ball of fear rattled in my throat, I could feel at the centre of my own existence a big hollow nothing which in normal boys would have been filled with courage. I had to do something to save myself, but what?

I don't remember exactly what happened next, except that when Glinda put her hand on my forehead, I felt all trembly.

'Are you sure you're alright, Kushenovitz?'

I didn't answer her; I ran out of that room as fast as I could, and I don't know where I was running to except maybe I was going to look for my voice.

I tell you, that rattle in my throat scared me. Sometimes when people are about to die, their breathing changes, and if you lean over and listen, you can hear this rattle in their throats – it's a sure sign that they are just about to kick the bucket. It's true – I've seen it in the movies.

That wasn't the first time I experienced that death-rattle. On the contrary, it's had a long history, dating way back.

It reached such a bad state with me, that I had the problem medically investigated when I was twelve. It might have had something to do with the strain put on my voice when I was studying to sing my barmitzvah.

'Ma, I've got something stuck in my throat!' I told her one day.

'I told you to chew properly. You always bolt your food.'

'Come off it, Ma, there's a bone stuck there. It's been there two months.'

'Let me look, Basil.'

She lifted my chin to the light and peered into the big hole.

'Nothing! But you're not brushing your teeth every day, are you?'

In the end my ma took me to Groote Schuur Hospital where they gave me moving X-rays – the kind where you can see the insides of your throat heaving as you swallow. It's like a movie, but it stars uvula and oesophagus and larynx, which is a lot better than Sylvester Stallone, but still not exactly thrilling. Of course, nothing was stuck in my throat and the ox of a doctor told me not to bolt my food in future, at which my ma smugly smiled her 'told you so' smile.

As my throat was supposedly in A1 condition, I had to continue barmitzvah lessons with Rabbi Podlus. I hated it; he tried to teach me the so-called tune of this piece of Old Testament, while I tried every which way to annoy him by getting it wrong. It made him hopping mad and in his pious way he would shout things at me like 'Du shtick dreck!', which roughly translated from Yiddish means 'You piece of shit.'

'You are not doing this for me, you know!' he would say. 'This is strictly between you and the ballaboss.'

Of course, to him the big-boss was God. But not only did I see no sign of the ballaboss, I couldn't even understand his Hebrew language. (I did check the translation once, but I got no further than the opening paragraph where Jehoash became king. Have you ever heard of Jehoash? Me neither.)

Eventually the great Saturday morning arrived, the day of my parents' great happiness. It was the first time I ever prayed in earnest.

'God,' I said, 'if you exist, and at this moment I don't want to offend you by doubting it, please help my nerves to calm down. Please inject at least one thimbleful of courage into me and keep the death-rattle away from my throat.'

When my prayer wasn't answered, I concluded quite logically that the ballaboss didn't exist – or else he only answered Hebrew prayers.

I can't tell you how nervous I was up there in front of the congregation. Let me just say that I sang the whole thing standing on one leg like a flamingo. Rabbi Podlus kept kicking my legs to make me stand properly, but only succeeded in making the lump in my throat rattle more forcefully, so that my voice wobbled like a strangled chicken.

That was when I turned thirteen. Before that, for six years, I used to go through the same nervousness every Passover festival. That's until my young brother Ivan grew up and was old enough to do the job. (It always has to be done by the youngest son present.)

Of course, the job was singing the Ma Nishtana. It was awful singing in front of the whole family: parents, grand-parents, aunts, uncles, cousins. Every year was spoiled by this one day where I was forced to sing in front of them all.

'Why is this night different from all other nights?' I used to sing, struggling with the rattle in my voicebox.

'Because tonight I have to sing this bladdy song in front of everybody,' I used to answer silently to myself.

The only person who had a worse time on Passover was our coloured servant Dolly. First of all she had to clean out all the crockery and cutlery beforehand, and get out the special Passover crockery and cutlery. But if that wasn't enough slaving around, she had to help my ma prepare this meal for God knows how many people, and then she had to spend the whole night serving the courses, bringing the food in and taking the empty plates back to the kitchen, and when it was all over, she had to load the dishwasher and clean up.

'Hey Dolly, bring more matzah!'

'Dolly, there should be more salt in the soup!'

'Dolly, please won't you bring another pillow from the bedroom for Uncle Harry to lean against.'

We were all supposed to sit in comfort around the laden table, to commemorate the time when Jews were slaves in Egypt, sweating blood to build the pyramids, while the Pharaoh's taskmasters whipped them, until eventually Moses came along and with the help of ten plagues, persuaded the Pharaoh to let his people go.

This was the very reason why my Uncle Jules never joined us for Passover dinner. (Actually, he never joined us for any dinner.)

'Can't you see, Basil, it's us whites who are the Pharaohs now, and the non-whites are the slaves who have built our skyscrapers? The only difference is that the non-white Moses was arrested for trying to liberate his people and had to spend most of his life in prison.'

No wonder Jules didn't get invited around for dinner.

Actually, the Moses from the Bible also had a voice problem like me; he was a nervous wreck when it came to speaking in front of Pharaohs and other people. But I'm not surprised in his case, because every now and again, voices would speak to him from burning bushes. That must be enough to scare the boots off anyone.

But what excuse do I have? I told you this death-rattle has a long history and I now must introduce you to a four-year-old boy, who was as cute as candyfloss. His mommy and his daddy loved him such a lot and they gave him everything he wanted.

They taught him to read and to write and they gave him lots of books, so that by the time he first went to kindergarten he was way ahead of the other kids, who hadn't even heard of this thing called the ABC. Mind you, when his dad left him there on his own the first day, he shat himself, and instantly learned that knowing the ABC doesn't help in all situations.

But there was this nice lady teacher called Miss Segal who thought he was the cutest kid in the school. She encouraged his verbal activities and pinned his written work on the classroom walls. Marvellous, wouldn't it be, to get this precocious boy to sing a delightful solo at the kindergarten concert?

So she taught him a song. And the song had a nice tune, but it was about a unicorn. And he didn't like unicorns, because they didn't exist. He wanted a song about a real animal like an elephant, but Miss Segal said 'No, this is a lovely song!'

On the night of the concert, this four-year-old boy was dressed up all cute with a little blue bowtie, so that he looked like a gift tied with a blue ribbon. Out he went to the front of the stage. And the audience clapped their welcome.

He searched the sea of faces for his mommy or his daddy or his grandfather or granny, but he couldn't see any of them. There were just hundreds of faces that didn't belong to anybody.

And there was a silence.

And Miss Segal nearly burst a blood vessel. 'Go on, sing!' she whispered. 'We're all waiting!'

And he could feel something rattling in his throat as he sang his song about the stupid unicorn.

And when it was finished, the audience clapped and he ran off backstage, thinking he had done very nicely.

But Miss Segal came up to him and said 'Basil, why did you sing so fast? You spoiled it all. You sang so fast and so softly that nobody could hear the words. Why didn't you do it like I taught you? All that preparation and you went and sang it twice as fast as you should have. It's a song, not a race! Why didn't you voice the words instead of just puffing them? Nobody could hear! Ai, yai, yai! Even I couldn't and I was standing right nearby! Everyone will be so disappointed with you!'

And why was this cute kid already afflicted with a death-rattle at only four years of age? To answer this, you would have had to know him one year earlier, after a severe bout of sinus, when he stopped eating for three weeks.

His daddy and his mommy were so worried about his loss of appetite, they made eating into a game.

'Here comes a helicopter!' they would say, and the spoonful of mashed pumpkin would fly round and round through the air, until suddenly 'It's landing!' they would shout, and the spoonful would land on his tongue. Uuuugh!

'And now a jumbo jet! Open up!'

The spoonful of mashed potato flew into his airport.

'Here's a really big one. It's Table Mountain!'

And the lump of mashed yellow squashie would come nearer and nearer to his mouth.

After each forcefeed, the kid left the table and ran down the passage to the toilet, where he bent over the pale turquoise bowl and vomited up endless helicopters and jumbo jets and mountain peaks.

Until one day.

He left the table.

He ran down the passage.

Into the toilet.

He bent over the turquoise bowl.

He started to vomit out helicopters and jumbo jets and mountains.

But halfway through . . .

'What the hell are you doing!'

He heard the monstrous voice, booming out above him. He turned his head towards the gigantic form standing at the toilet door. He could see it from its toes to the level of its neck, but he didn't want to lift his eyes to look into its face.

It was his daddy, huge and ferocious, a giant, standing at the toilet door, looking down at the wicked little boy who had attempted to deceive him.

'How dare you pretend to eat and then come here and vomit it all up? All that precious food. Other people in Africa are starving. Your mommy and me take such trouble to make those shapes for you to eat. And what do you do? You come here and vomit it up.'

The little boy stopped himself vomiting. Table Mountain was stuck halfway up his throat. It was a painful lump rattling from side to side.

The giant was furious.

'You won't ever vomit your food again, will you?'

'N . . . n . . . n . . . n . . . o, D . . . d . . . d . . . d . . . daddy.'

Until then the three-year-old boy had never even dreamed that sin could exist. He had never done anything wrong, never known anything *could* be wrong. His every action, his every thought had been pure and innocent. He lived in a world of unending bliss – until his almighty father caught him in that toilet. Vomiting up food was his original sin, and in that moment of being discovered, he was mercilessly evicted from paradise, like an illegal squatter.

And he was never allowed back in.

So you see, it was a clear case of one thing leading to

another. From being a three-year-old boy, one thing led to another, and now I've grown into an eighteen-year-old.

But if I were to be honest I would have to admit that I've still got a very strong bond with that boy who was cast out from paradise with a ball of fear and vomit still stuck in his throat. Truly, that pikkie and I have such a strange relationship – sometimes it feels like I play games with him, or converse with him, or go walking with him, leading him by the hand wherever I go. Or is he leading me? Difficult to tell, isn't it?

Mr Naidoo's hundredth birthday

In my last year of school I had a Saturday morning job at Valhalla Furniture. I worked mainly in the lighting department, demonstrating various lamps and light fittings for customers. My head was so filled with details of watts and volts, I'm sure it would have shone in the dark like a chandelier.

Naturally, I didn't do this job out of my own choice – I had better things to do on a Saturday morning than bringing light into people's lives. But my dad insisted I did this work. And it was he also who was responsible for the lousy pay I received. But what could I do about it? He owned Valhalla Furniture.

Working on that job I got to know Boola quite well. But really I think you have to put yourself in someone else's skin before you can understand them properly, wouldn't you say? All the more so if their skin is a different colour to yours. At any rate, that's what my ma always says about the handicapped people she works with at the Woltemade Centre.

Old Boola had been handyman at Valhalla Furniture for years; he was quite good with hammer and nails and a woodsaw. All furniture assembly and such things were left for Boola, though he actually fancied himself as a bit of a sweet-talking salesman, and was always trying to get a piece of the sales action. I think he reckoned he could talk a man with no wife into buying a double bed, but as far as I know the closest he ever came to that was talking some old sailor into buying a rocking chair to remind him of the ocean waves.

My ma always took time to talk to Boola, on her brief visits to Valhalla.

'How's Meena doing?' she would ask every time.

I suppose my ma was interested in Boola's daughter because of her work with handicapped people. From what I could gather, Meena was a bit retarded.

'She's okay, Missus, but she struggles with the children, you know.'

'Is it four children?'

'It's five now, Missus.'

'Ag, shame,' my ma would say. 'What about a husband for her?'

'No, Missus, the men just take advantage of her, but they don't want to marry someone like her, even though she's got a heart of gold, I tell you.'

'Can't you arrange a marriage for her?'

'I've tried, Missus, but the only man I could get had a messed-up face.'

'What do you mean?'

'He was in a car accident and his face is very bad. No woman can look at him.'

'Did Meena meet him?'

'Yes, Missus, she said he was a nice man, very kind, and she would marry him, but after he spoke to her, he said to me he didn't want to marry a halfwit person.'

'Ag shame,' my ma said.

Boola struggled hard to support Meena and the children. He lived with them in some little house in the back of Retreat. I suppose that's why he tried to get in on the sales action, to earn a bit of commission.

But it became harder and harder to sell anything at

Valhalla Furniture. Even the real salesmen were having trouble.

It was all the fault of the Portuguese opposite. They started up the Discount Furniture Centre in the huge Newgate shopping precinct that got built across the road from Valhalla. And my dad had to watch for three years how those guys built up their business, while those guys watched him going down the drain. They were ruthless, and reclaimed furniture after the first lapse of payment. You could see their heavies going out in their brand new vans and returning with the almost new furniture. Whereas my dad did his debt-collecting mostly on his own. One Saturday morning he took me with him.

I sat in our trusty old van as he knocked on the front door of this tin-roofed house in Plumstead. A huge man with a red face came to the door and I heard my dad explaining the situation to him. But he couldn't have explained it too well, because the red-faced chap started gesticulating with both his enormous hands.

'A man's got to eat!' he screamed.

I thought what a pity my dad disturbed him during his meal.

'You think all I've got to do is pay you for that shitty table you sold us? Come in and see it, man, it's falling to bits.'

I wasn't surprised: if one of those gesticulations made contact with that table during a meal, it wouldn't have stood a chance. Nor would my dad's face, if he argued much longer.

'I didn't want that table in the first place. It's your salesman who told me I need to eat on a dining table. There was nothing wrong with my old kitchen table. If you can't wait another month, you can take back your piece of shit and shove it up your Jew-arse.'

Well, of course, in the end my dad was persuaded by those eloquent words and gesticulations to take pity on the man, and I don't know if he ever got paid for that table.

Meanwhile the Portuguese got richer and richer, and even our longstanding customers started frequenting the Discount Centre opposite. My dad would surely have developed ulcers had he gone on watching such ruthless men thrive while his own business went to the dogs. But the bankruptcy came quickly and was over and done in a jiffy, and soon after, my dad got the job at the Plaza cinema, and he's never looked back, because he's always loved films and knows who acts in every one and who wrote the music and who directed it and so on.

But when Valhalla started getting into its troubles, Boola was very anxious about losing his job.

'Who will look after my daughter and my grandchildren, Boss Kush?' he asked my dad.

My dad had no answer, because you tell me, who's going to employ a shabbily dressed sixty-three-year-old Indian whose sweet-talking mouth dribbles saliva every now and again?

The last straw at Valhalla was the burglary. There had been a spate of shop burglaries nearby that had my dad seriously worried, because he knew Valhalla didn't have the most modern security. In fact, it didn't have security at all, because what my dad had done was to lay these wires across all the shop windows himself, as if they were a proper burglar alarm system. But the wires all went to this phoney board of electrical apparatus that he found somewhere, and it wasn't plugged into anything! The pretence was completed by this metal sign which he managed to get hold of and which read 'THIS PROPERTY IS PROTECTED BY TRIDENT SECURITY SYSTEMS.'

This pretence had obviously worked for the seven years my dad owned Valhalla, because it had never been burgled. He also had a lot of faith in the fact that the police station was just down the road. But these particular burglars must have had no respect for the police being so nearby, and they also weren't fooled by the sign. They stole thousands of rands worth of goods, mostly small furniture items, light fittings and rugs – it must have been well-planned – and what's more, they even stole the metal Trident Security Systems sign.

My dad lost a lot of money, because the insurance company wouldn't pay up once they discovered my dad's so-called security system. It was an awful morning, standing there in an half-empty shop, realizing that the end had come. And it was all the more awful knowing the Portuguese across the road were watching and gloating at your misfortune.

But Boola wasn't there to see the end.

It's funny, now I look back on all the time Boola worked for my dad, I would never have guessed that he was the sort of person to do what he did. Even though once or twice I spoke to him about his life.

I remember once old Boola asked me about the Woltemade Centre where my ma worked. I think maybe he secretly wanted to know if they could help his daughter Meena in any way. In passing, I told him that the centre was named after this bloke Wolraad Woltemade, who rode out into the raging waves to save the lives of sailors who were shipwrecked in Table Bay a long time ago. Time after time he rode out, returning with desperate sailors clinging to his horse. Until his horse tired, and both man and beast sank beneath the waves.

'That's a smart story, Master Basil,' he said. 'You will be a good journalist. Then you must tell a smart story about me, hey?'

'What must I tell?'

'You can tell that Boola got his Standard 8 and then he worked for twenty-five years for Mr Swersky selling bicycles, and eighteen years for Mr Leopold making picture frames, and then for your father another seven years in the furniture trade.'

'That's not enough for a story,' I said.

'Man, it was enough for a life. Why not for a story?'

'Didn't anything interesting ever happen to you?'

'Of course, what do you think I am? Now let me remember.'

But old Boola's memories weren't so good, I reckon, because the best he could come up with, was something about marrying a no-good girl who ran off with a coloured man, leaving him with a simple-minded daughter.

'And I've got good Indian and Malay blood in me, not like that bleddy Hotnot she ran off with!'

But on that occasion I never guessed what Boola had done. Nor another time long ago, when I must have been about twelve or so, and Boola helped me with my school woodwork project.

I had decided to make a wooden jigsaw puzzle with this great picture I had – actually it was a poster – of surfriders. I stuck it on to some plywood with glue, then drew the outlines of all the pieces on the back. But my attempts at using the fretsaw were abysmal.

'You can't use such a blunt blade!' Boola told me, when I showed him my efforts. 'This blade is smooth as a baby's bum.'

It looked sharp enough to me, but he ran his leathery old thumb over the blade to prove the point.

So I went to the hardware shop and bought a new pack of blades.

'This is how you use a fretsaw,' Boola said. 'You keep the blade moving steady like this, see, and you keep the blade nice and upright.'

I tried, but still my pieces chipped as I turned the corner.

In the end Boola did half of the sawing, and I did the other half.

'Hey, that's fine handiwork, hey!'

The jigsaw was great. There were 200 pieces of complicated puzzle, which would give anybody a hard time. Old Forbesy liked my work and gave me a good mark. Much better than the mark I got for making my perspex matchbox holder the year before.

Yes, looking back, it is easy to see that even while Boola was helping me with that jigsaw, I had no idea of the person who was sitting there so kindly helping me.

I only found out when these two men turned up in the lighting department at Valhalla and asked to see Mr Gopal Naidoo.

'We're from the Municipality of Cape Town,' the one man said. He was dressed in a smart, charcoal pinstriped suit.

'No Mr Gopal Naidoo works here,' I said.

'Are you sure?' the other man chimed in. His suit was navy blue, and he was carrying a box wrapped in shiny gold paper. 'Where's the manager of this place?'

'My father's the manager,' I said. 'Come with me.'

As they walked behind me, Mr Charcoal whispered to Mr Navyblue.

'You see, I told you he couldn't be at this place. That woman was halfwitted, man. She didn't even know her own name.'

When we reached my dad's partitioned-off office, he told them that there was no Mr Gopal Naidoo in his employ. Only a Mr Boola Naidoo.

Mr Navyblue raised his eyebrows.

'Did he used to work in the Parks Department?' he asked.

'I doubt it,' my dad said. 'He's been a handyman for years. I don't think he knows the first thing about gardening.'

'He didn't work as a gardener,' Mr Navyblue explained. 'He worked as a cleaner.'

'We better have a word with this Boola Naidoo!' Mr Charcoal said.

Boola came into the office, smiling and showing his brown teeth.

'Are you Mr Boola Naidoo?' Mr Charcoal asked.

'That's me,' Boola said.

'Do you know a Mr Gopal Naidoo?' Mr Navyblue asked.

'Yes, sir, that's my father.'

'Excellent,' Mr Navyblue said. 'We have been trying to locate him. We've got an address in Retreat for him, but when we got there, this woman told us he wasn't there, and we should try Valhalla Furniture. Where exactly can we find him?'

'Why you want to see him?' Boola asked.

'We understand the old boy is 100 years old today,' Mr Charcoal explained, 'so we have come to give him this gift and a certificate signed by the Mayor of Cape Town himself.'

'Thank you,' Boola said. 'I will give it to him.'

'That's good of you, but we need to have a photograph of your father receiving the award.'

'My father is not well,' Boola said. 'He's very ill. He cannot have a photograph.'

'I'm sorry he's not well,' Mr Charcoal said. 'But where is he at the moment?'

Boola had the look on his face like he was trying to sell a double bed to a man with no wife.

'He's . . . he's . . . he's at my brother's house in Port Elizabeth.'

'So when he claims his pension every month,' Mr Charcoal said, 'why does he give the address in Retreat?'

'Because . . . because . . .' Boola wasn't having any luck selling his double bed. 'Because he always lives in Retreat except now when he is so ill. I send the money to him in Port Elizabeth.'

Mr Charcoal turned again to Mr Navyblue.

'There's some fishy business going on over here, don't you think?'

'Ja, I smell a rat,' Mr Navyblue answered.

'Look here, Mr Naidoo, the Municipality has been paying out a pension to Mr Gopal Naidoo for thirty-five years and for thirty-five years he has put his thumbprint on our claim forms. According to our records, he is 100 years old today. So we've come to pay him the respects of the Municipality and to give him this nice box of gifts and a certificate, but if he's in Port Elizabeth, then you tell me, how has he been filling in his claim form?'

Poor old Boola didn't know what to say.

'It's a serious offence to forge a pension claim,' Mr Navyblue said.

'But what about the thumbprint?' my father said. 'You can't forge a thumbprint.'

'I think we'll take another ride to Retreat,' Mr Charcoal said, 'and you can come with us, Mr Naidoo.'

Old Boola bowed his head pathetically, and went off with the two men.

'I can't leave the shop,' my dad said to me, 'but let's get hold of your mom.'

He made a quick phone call and within ten minutes my ma had collected me and we were off to Retreat to see if Boola needed help.

Once we found the street, it was easy to see which was Boola's little house. It was the one with the shiny black Ford from the Municipality parked outside.

We knocked on the door and this short plump lady in a shabby, worn-out pink dress answered.

'Yes, Boola is here,' she said, in a sweet child's voice. 'But he is talking to someone.'

'We will also talk to him, Meena,' my ma said, taking her confidently by the arm and leading her indoors.

The house was so small, just a front room and two back rooms and a kitchen. Two barefoot children were sitting on the floor of the front room, their noses runny and their clothes ragged. On the wall behind the couch was a faded picture of an elephant with many arms. The settee itself was covered with a large cloth, that might once have been

66

an old curtain. On it Boola was sitting. He was hardly able to greet my ma.

I could hear the voices of Mr Charcoal and Mr Navyblue coming from one of the back rooms.

Meena sat down next to Boola. My ma and me kept standing.

'Why are those men looking in the room, Boola?' Meena asked him.

'They're just looking for papers,' Boola said.

Suddenly, the two men emerged. Mr Charcoal was triumphantly holding up a jar in his hands, well away from his nose, which appeared to be suffering from the effects of a noxious smell.

If they were surprised to see my ma and me in that house, they didn't show it. Mr Charcoal just held up the jar and I could see it contained liquid.

'I'd like you to meet what is left of the 100 year-old Mr Gopal Naidoo!' Mr Charcoal said, giving us a closer look at the jar.

I couldn't believe it.

There in the liquid was an ancient old thumb.

The thumb of Mr Gopal Naidoo, Boola's father, deceased twenty-something years ago.

My ma remained silent.

Boola held his head down. He knew he was in big trouble.

'This is a serious offence, Mr Naidoo,' Mr Navyblue said. 'You will be hearing from us and the police in due course.'

Mr Charcoal and Mr Navyblue strutted off, pleased with their day's work.

'What was in the bottle, Boola?' Meena asked.

'It was our life's savings,' Boola answered her gently, putting his arm around her.

Pondokkie

We didn't use to visit Jules very often. Maybe once a year, if my dad got an attack of family feeling. You see, Jules was my dad's youngest brother, and was a bit of a failure in life, and if there's one thing that gets my dad's goat, it's failure.

My dad's other brother, Leon, was a different story: him and his family we used to visit often, because he had gone through university to become an engineer with his own factory for producing this new type of tip-up garage door. We had some of his Eezy-Lift doors on our garage, and I must say, they had a very smooth action – the sort of smooth action that twice a day reminded my dad to tell me how valuable a university education would be.

But Jules was a failure. He couldn't have used a free sample of Eezy-Lift garage doors at his house, because he didn't even have a garage. For a long time he didn't even have a car. Then he bought this beaten up Marina jalopy and he used to go touring the Cape to find good subjects to paint.

I liked his paintings, but I must have been the only person in the Cape Province who did, because he hardly ever sold any. The reason I liked them was because you could see all these subtle colours in each face. If you held the portrait towards the windows, the expression on the face would change ever so slightly, as the colours brightened or dimmed. I think each colour was something he saw in that person's personality.

His house was in Hout Bay, overlooking the curved shoreline and the little harbour. But he never painted landscapes.

'Why don't you paint what you see from your own window?' my dad asked him repeatedly. 'That's what people want, pretty pictures of the coast and the boats.'

'It's not my thing,' Jules would answer, and he remained poor.

After our rare visits to him my dad would usually come up with some comment like 'He walks around in sandals and those broken trousers, just like a shoch. He's got no education. He's wasted his life, that man, living there on his own like a hermit.'

But I liked Jules. He had a rough shaggy beard, just like Van Gogh, except he still had both ears. And instead of a Dutch straw hat, he always wore a conical shaped Basuto straw hat, that he picked up somewhere on one of his travels.

I was convinced that one day Jules would be famous and then my dad would be proud of him after all. But that day seemed a long time coming and the only thing he accumulated were his watercolour paintings. They lay around the house like my brother Ivan's old comics.

The rooms of Jules's house contained the bare minimum of furniture: a table and chair in the kitchen, an old bed and cupboard in one room, and two easy chairs, with their stuffing hanging out below, in what must have been the sitting room.

'That's not a house,' my dad would say after a visit, 'it's a pondokkie. I'm ashamed to go in there.'

He must have been very ashamed, because he never spent more than two and a half minutes indoors. Then he would ask Jules if he wanted to come and have a picnic with us on the white sands. Sometimes Jules agreed, other times he was too involved in a painting to bother with picnics and family obligations. Then my dad would go off the handle on the way home.

'Bladdy unsociable person! Who would think that's my own brother? My own flesh and blood? We drive all the way to see him and he can't be bothered to say two civil words to us. He's more interested in his paintings of non-whites. And his pondokkie stinks.'

My dad has never liked pondokkies.

I remember one incident so clearly that shows my dad's attitude to pondokkies. It happened when I was about nine years old just after the Coleman's house caught fire and burnt down.

Everyone in the area saw the black smoke ladling up into the sky and ran to watch. By the time I got there it was nearly all over. The firemen were running around busily like they were doing something, but they were just hosing water into this burnt-out shell of a house. There was, I remember, a strange collection of items salvaged on the lawn, including a golf bag filled with clubs. And I remember Mr Coleman's arm, covered with black ash, trying to comfort Mrs Coleman who wept unashamedly.

Of course, the Coleman's rebuilt their house with the insurance money, and many people said they did darn well out of it too, because the new house was far more spacious than the old one, but that's another story.

Our house was called 'Tallis'. My dad said it was a Greek name for a gateway to the gods. He gave it that name because from our house you can see the back of Table Mountain, and its granite walls stretch up so high it looks as if the gods could live up there, if there were such things as gods. Especially after it rains and the waterfalls burst out of those granite walls like a balloon that's been punctured in a few places. Ja, I'm sure if the gods wanted a good place to live, they couldn't do much better than on the top of that mountain.

It was easy to think of our house as the gateway. Anybody wanting to go visiting gods up that mountain would have to first stop at our place and be checked out – see that they've got the proper papers to go visiting gods, and maybe pay the gateman a small fee. Of course, any of the houses in our road, or our suburb, or any of the suburbs around the foot of Table Mountain could have called themselves 'Tallis' and then they could have collected the small fee. But my dad thought of the idea first, so I think he was entitled to a rand now and again.

My grandfather was really pleased with my dad for calling the house 'Tallis'. He has always been very religious, and he thought my dad was giving the house the name for the Jewish prayer shawl.

'Ai, Max, what a lovely name!'

Even though I was so young, I couldn't see myself why a house should have the name of a prayer shawl – I mean, it's like calling a house 'Scarf' or 'Doekie' or 'Raincoat' – so I could understand when my dad used to change the subject whenever my grandfather mentioned it.

For me, at that time, it was always gateway to the gods, even though my dad used to warn me never to go walking near the foot of the mountain. In fact, he didn't even like me walking to the bottom end of the road, because just beyond it was the Liesbeek River. It was just a piddly stream down there, as it was still so near its source on Table Mountain. Only once it reached Liesbeek Park or thereabouts, could it be considered a proper river.

When it rained though, the stream could grow in size very rapidly, and occasionally it swelled over its banks and flooded my main playing area by the mimosa trees.

I remember I used to play there with my friend Dewie mostly, though occasionally we let smarty-pants Rodney come along for the fun of it. He was such a drip; he would always get himself wet, even if we kept well away from the river. I don't honestly know how he managed it; I think maybe sometimes it just used to rain on Rodney and on no one else. But he regularly went home wet and tried to talk his way out of a punishment from his ma, who was furious with him for playing by the Liesbeek River.

Personally, I never got caught out for playing by the Liesbeek until this one day. And I never got wet either until that same day.

On that occasion, Dewie didn't want to come down with me to the river because he had been given stilts for his birthday and wanted to try them out. I would have stayed with him to have a go as well, but after I saw how distant they were from the ground, I thought it would be fairer if Dewie tried out his own birthday present first. Also, giving myself a day or two to grow before trying out such high stilts didn't seem such a bad idea to me.

When I got to the patch of mimosas, I played in the bushes as usual. And I would never have got wet if I hadn't seen this smoke coming from the other side of the Liesbeek. I had to go investigate, of course, because fires could be dangerous.

The only way over the river was to use stepping stones. There were quite a few sets of stepping stones over the Liesbeek, but there was one I preferred, which I kept in good repair. Every time one of the gaps seemed too big, I used to lug across a big stone and drop it in at the right place so that most times it was easy for me to cross that river back and forth, except after heavy rain when my stepping stones disappeared so far beneath the surface, you couldn't even see them.

The veld wasn't on fire at all. It was someone making a braaivleis, except it wasn't meat he was braaing, it was fish – small fish the size of sardines. I never saw anyone braai fish like that before then and I've never seen it since, except for me. Once or twice I tried to braai sardines in my backyard, but I didn't let anyone see me doing it.

But this man didn't mind at all. He had all the fish

threaded on a piece of wire held up on either side by two twigs. It was the same method you would use if you wanted to roast a pig – that is, if you're not Jewish, of course. This man couldn't have been Jewish, because his skin wasn't white and his hair grew in little clumps on his head like a coloured.

When he saw me, I came to a dead stop. I didn't move. Nor did he. Not even one eyelid. Maybe he was scared of me also. If it wasn't for his fish cooking, maybe we would have stayed there without moving all day. But his fish started sizzling, and they would have shrivelled up into little burnt skeletons, if he hadn't've moved. So he moved. He lifted the wire off the twigs and in one movement, just as if he was playing cards, he dealt them all on to his orange plastic plate.

Then he lifted his plate to me and said 'Want one?'

I wasn't hungry, because I had already started my day with a good helping of Pro-Nutro. But the way he offered me that small fish, I got the feeling he'd be disappointed if I didn't share them with him. Also it would stop him being so scared of me. So I took one grilled fish off the plate and nearly burnt my hands. He gave me a small version of his orange plastic plate to put it on, and then he slid two more fish on to my plate.

They were massively tasty; so much so, that I decided one day I would grill some sardines at home on our braai in the backyard.

While we were eating I watched his face, with its wrinkles and brown colours, but we didn't say anything. I also noticed he didn't mind if his clothes were a bit torn. My ma would have given me hell if I came back with my shirt ripped the way his was, or with shoes torn so that the baby toe stuck out, or if I lost my socks. Ma also would have done her nut if my fingernails were like his, black and long like a woman's. But he didn't seem to mind much.

He washed down his fish with this blue drink from a

bottle, I didn't know what it was at the time. I remember it looked to me like paraffin or the methylated spirits that my dad kept in the garage, but of course I thought it couldn't have been, because my only experience was of those things being used for machines and cleaning things, and nobody would drink such a liquid, would they? I reckoned it was possibly some new brandy or something, but I wouldn't have known, because obviously, at that time, I'd never touched a drop of brandy in my life.

Right through breakfast I was admiring his little pondokkie. Often Dewie and I made huts near the mimosa patch, but they were just pretend. This man's hut was real. It was made of branches and a couple of old pieces of corrugated iron and looked like it would give good shelter even in a rain.

After breakfast the man said I could look in his house. It was a good hut, that's for sure, with one pan hanging on the wall, and one little chopper. I remember it so clearly; it had a musty smell of old clothes. On the ground on one side of the hut was a sack which was his bed. I couldn't see a pillow, or pyjamas, but I reckoned as he was camping alone, he didn't need those luxuries.

'Ja, ja,' he kept saying. 'Home sweet home, hey?'

I had to agree.

Then he got some string out of this bag in his hut and he got the chopper and he walked over to a clump of bushes. He bent two larger branches so as to make a big semi-circle and he showed me how to bind them together with a reef knot.

'No grannies, hey!' he said. 'Otherwise your hut falls to pieces if you fart.'

He cackled to himself as he tied more and more branches into this beehive shape, chopping a branch here, a branch there, sticking branches firmly into the ground here and there, until the whole thing was looking pretty tight. Then he positioned a few small scraps of corrugated iron in the roof, and wove branches in a criss-cross direction around them until not even light could get through the roof.

'Jeez, I must show Dewie this hut, when he's finished playing with his stilts.'

'Ja, you can bring him if you want.'

When it was completed, I went and sat inside. It was fantastic. It was like sitting inside an egg in the middle of the veld. That's what a bird must feel like in its egg, I thought.

'Now you know how to do it,' the man said. 'You can make one yourself tomorrow or the next day or the day that never comes.'

I didn't know which day never comes, but I thought I would try and make my own hut one day, if I could get hold of a chopper.

The man came and sat with me in the hut he made for me and he drank some more of his blue brandy.

Then he pulled out this dirty pack of cards and he said 'I'll teach you a game, hey?'

He separated the pack into two piles. 'We only use these cards. Now I deal you out a hand and me also . . .'

'What's this game called?' I asked him.

'Klawerjas,' he said.

'Klabberjas?' I said. I thought I recognized the game. My grandfather had taught it to me. 'I can play klabberjas.'

'Let's see,' he said.

As he dealt, I wondered how he had learned to play a Jewish game, and if he could play it properly. He told me my rules were wrong a few times, and I told him his rules were wrong, but somehow we managed to compromise.

We could have sat there playing all day, for sure, but I heard this voice calling 'Bazzie! Bazzie!'

My name is Basil and there's only one person who calls me Bazzie sometimes and that's my dad; I knew I was in for trouble.

'I'm here!' I answered. 'In this hut.'

My father came across the stepping stones and poked his head in my hut.

'What are you doing there? God, what are you doing with this skollie here? Get out of there!'

His long arm reached into the hut and I felt my shirt tear as he pulled me out in one movement. The klabberjas cards went flying. Dewie's dad, Mr Getz, was also standing there with a knobkierie in his one hand.

'Go back home!' my dad screamed at me. 'I've told you never to come down here!'

My dad's rage isn't something that you can argue with; it's like a storm. You just have to let the rain and the wind blow down on you for hours until it's over. Unless you can find Ma's shelter to protect you for a while. And Mr Getz's temper was even more violent; everyone in our neighbourhood knew that.

So I started walking back over my stepping stones.

I could hear my dad and Mr Getz screaming at Skollie.

'You bladdy drunkard! You leave our children alone! What's this bladdy rubbish you drinking? This stuff will burn your insides out! It will make you blind and kill you, don't you know!'

I turned round to see Mr Getz pouring out Skollie's blue brandy on to the ground and my dad kicking down my pondokkie.

It was then that I fell in the water and got wet in the Liesbeek River for the first and last time ever. I kept my eyes on the two white men. The storm wasn't over yet. Mr Getz started ripping down Skollie's own hut, even though it had his bed in it and a frying pan hanging on the wall. And I don't think Skollie could claim on his insurance policy, the way the Coleman's had.

Mr Getz was about to start on Skollie with his knobkierie, but my dad came between them and started yelling.

'You not allowed to live down here! You can't just live

wherever you want! This is a white area. Go find some-where else to live, man!'

Skollie hobbled off hastily in the opposite direction, swearing to himself.

The two men watched him disappear then turned round to head for home also. I reached the other side of the river, thinking that now the storm was finished with Skollie, it would be my turn next, so I started to run like hell. I ran through the mimosa patch and up the high bank to the bottom of my road, and then I ran all the way up my road nonstop.

Dewie was doing well on his stilts. From that height he could almost see over the three metre high wall, topped with lethal glass shards, that surrounded his own house. I didn't even stop to tell Dewie that I knew a good way of making a strong hut, and he had to move fast on his high stilts to get out of my way.

'What's the hurry, Baz? Your dad's looking for you, you know!'

I looked round. Dewie's dad and my dad were at the bottom of the road, moving at a fast pace.

Eventually I got to our house and in through the front gate under the sign 'Tallis'. Then up the stairs to our stoep and in through the front door. Ma was cooking supper in the kitchen and I went to sit with her even though I knew she'd be mad with me for my wet clothes and torn shirt.

I still remember as my ma hugged me that day, I thought of Skollie and I thought maybe I'd go and tell him the next day that the only good place to build his pondokkie would be on the flat top of Table Mountain. But of course I was just a youngster and didn't know that in South Africa even the gods would need permits to live in one group area or another.

Yes, my dad wasn't too keen on pondokkies in those days, or hermits, for that matter – nor more recently, as he proved when the letter arrived from his brother, Jules.

It came as a total surprise to us, out of the blue. There was this letter from Jules saying that he was driving up to Joburg for the opening of an exhibition and would I like to accompany him on the journey? I must have been about fifteen then.

'No way are you going with that hermit!' my dad said.

But I was quite keen. It wasn't only Jules's paintings that I liked: I also liked him. He seemed to me to be a gentle person, but strong inside himself. I didn't know too many people like that.

For about ten days my dad and ma argued the pros and cons of my being allowed to go with. Suddenly it seemed that Jules was the most dangerous person in the world for a fifteen-year-old to associate with. All my parents' paranoias came out in the open that week: until then I didn't even know that they could have such grotesque fears lurking in their usually quite liberal minds.

'His jalopy will never reach Joburg,' my dad said.

'Does he even drive safely?' my ma asked.

'He'll probably try to convince Bazzie that possessions are capitalist evils,' my dad said.

'I'm just worried that he won't look after Basil properly,' my ma said. 'Jules looks like he never eats.'

'What if he's become perverted after all these years,' my dad said.

'Oh my God, do you mean homosexual?' my ma asked.

'Well, he's lived alone for so long, there must be something wrong with him.'

'He might try to persuade Basil not to go to university.'

'Or turn him against us, have you thought of that?' my dad said to my ma.

'Or turn him into a Communist.'

'Or even worse.'

'What's worse?'

'I don't know, they might both get arrested for stirring up trouble.'

I just let them get rid of all their wind and held my nose for those ten days. Then I told them I wanted to go, that I could look after myself, that I liked Jules, that it would be good for my future career in journalism to go up to Joburg for the opening of an exhibition.

'I can't believe he's having an exhibition!' my dad said. 'What gallery would be interested in his dabblings?'

On the Friday morning, Jules's Marina turned up outside our house as arranged.

My parents and me said our goodbyes.

'You'll take care, won't you?' my ma said.

'He'll be alright,' my dad said, hugging her. 'He's nearly a man now, and besides, even if Julie is a bit of a meshugena, he is still my brother.'

Of course, my parents were just paranoid. Jules was perfectly civil with me all the way. He explained that his exhibition was called 'Cape Flats', partly because of the way he exploited flat space in each watercolour, but also because each was developed from sketches he'd made in the Cape Flats.

'Those Cape Flats are truly barren and flat,' he told me. 'You would even have to bribe a tree to grow there, that's for sure.'

He explained to me that the government were the only people who had a special fondness for the Cape Flats. They reckoned that the Cape Flats were so huge and barren and sandy and flat, you could house hundreds of thousands of non-whites there, without too much bother. All you had to do was provide a few four-square-wall pondokkies and one tap, and hey presto, you've got a new residential area!

'The trouble was,' Jules went on, 'even though the area was as barren as a eunuch's future, there were thousands of non-whites who were desperate enough to *want* to live there. They came from far and wide, seeking work in Cape Town, but because they were there illegally, they resorted to squatting in makeshift dilapidated shacks. After a while the army moved in, and knocked their shelters down. But the squatters rebuilt them. Again they were knocked down, and rebuilt. Eventually the squatters got into the habit of knocking down their own shacks in the morning, to save the army trouble, and rebuilt them every evening. This really annoyed the army which finally levelled the whole area to the ground and forcibly removed the squatters from the Cape Town area altogether.'

It turned out the Zenobia Gallery was really posh and Jules was treated like a celebrity. My dad should have been there to see. The paintings of those poor squatters were hung on all four walls of the gallery and it spoke more eloquently than journalism ever could about the plight of those unfortunate people.

How odd it was to see all these wealthy white art patrons, dripping with diamond and gold jewellery, examining the heartrending images spread out before them. I don't know if they were moved by them or not. I mostly heard comments like 'Reminds one of Cezanne,' or 'Very good colour. Do you think it will go with the curtains?'

Jules sold quite a few paintings and that was just as well, because the old Marina packed up on the way to the opening, and nothing would induce it to move again. We went back to Cape Town by train.

I was pleased though, to read one critic's review of the exhibition. After mentioning the relevance and poignancy of Jules Kushenovitz's vision, it went on about his sense of colour and how the subtle tones in the portraits reflected elements of each subject's personality.

Jules is quite famous now, even my dad says so, but he still doesn't like to visit him in his old pondokkie in Hout Bay. The only concession my dad has made is in connection with this one watercolour which Jules had given us several years ago. My dad extricated it from a box of junk he kept in the roof, and now it hangs on the wall in our passage.

How Table Mountain got its cloth

What would most people do if they were walking along and they found a discarded handbag under a hedge and in it were a pair of diamond earrings and matching necklace?

I think what one would find most difficult in those circumstances would be to stop oneself from screaming 'I'm rich! Thank you God almighty!' and dancing with joy in the street.

Probably what most people would do, in fact, would be to walk off with the handbag as quickly as possible – not too quickly or people might notice – until they got home. Then they could scream about newly acquired wealth to their heart's content.

The only reason I mention this situation is because that is what happened to Dolly last year.

And it shows you what kind of a person she is, because after finding the jewels, she looked through the rest of the handbag, found some plastic bank cards and a diary, and worked out who the bag belonged to and the address of its owner.

Dolly then went to that address, which was in the neighbourhood, and rang the bell.

A lady about fifty-something years old opened it.

'Excuse, Missus,' Dolly said.

'My bag!' the woman exclaimed, her cheeks flushing all colours of the rainbow, one after the other. 'Where did you find my bag! I've just notified the police! God, I thought it was gone forever! A man snatched it right off my arm in Dorchester Avenue. He cut the strap, look! My heart! My blood pressure! I nearly died when he pulled it off. But where did you find it, you wonderful girl!'

The woman checked the contents.

'Thank God, the jewellery is there. But where's my purse? You didn't see my purse? My money has been stolen.'

The woman looked like she was going to have a heart attack on the spot, but eventually she calmed down and remembered Dolly who was standing there patiently on her front doorstep.

'Wait there, my girl, you deserve something for returning this to me.'

She retreated indoors, then returned a couple of minutes later with two ten rand notes.

'That's for you, my girl,' the woman said. 'Thank you very much.'

'Thank you, Missus,' Dolly said.

The next day, my ma read in the *Cape Times* that a Mrs Kraichik had been robbed in Bishopscourt in broad daylight. The thief had stolen her purse containing fifty rands, but ignored her earrings and matching necklace, worth over 14,000 rands. These, the article said, had been returned to Mrs Kraichik by an anonymous coloured woman, who had found the discarded bag under a hedge.

'And all she gave you, Dolly, was twenty rands,' my ma said. 'She must be a stingy old cow.'

But it shows you the kind of person that Dolly was, doesn't it, even if she had no idea at the time how valuable those jewels were.

Dolly has worked for our family seven years now, and most of that time she seemed contented, as far as I could tell. Except that she had a very low opinion of herself.

'My younger sister, Betty, she works in O.K. Bazaars as a

assistant. My brother, Herman, he works in the Standard
Bank on the counter. But me I'm too stupid to work in the
town.'

Her only hope, she said, was to marry someone with a
good job, otherwise she'd be a servant all her life.

Dolly cooked for us, and cleaned for us, for over seven
years, and the only thing I ever heard her complain about
was cigar and pipe ash on the carpets and the settee.

My dad has always smoked cigars. How well I remember
those drives all over the Peninsula with the smoke from his
cigar filling the whole car. Of course, it wasn't so bad in
summer, when the windows were open, but in winter,
when the constant rain depressed everyone's spirits and
the cold weather meant that the car windows had to be
shut, it was a different proposition.

The car filled with acrid cigar smoke and my ma and Ivan
and me had to put up with it the whole journey. How my
dad saw out the windows to drive was beyond human
understanding, because the smoke was thick, thick, thick.
Talk about getting stuck in a fog, we used to carry our own
fog with us, and wherever we went, it went. It was like the
pillar of smoke in the Bible leading Moses through the
desert, except that the smoke in our car was leading us
nowhere fast and made us all so irritable that we spent the
entire drive coughing, spluttering and finding the scenery
miserable. Of course it was miserable – we could hardly see
it because of smoke!

But I'll say one thing for my dad. He never inhaled. He
said it was bad for the lungs. The only drawback was *I*
didn't know how to breathe without inhaling. So I don't
suppose my lungs benefited from my dad's not inhaling.

Anyway, cigar smoke is not as bad as pipe smoke,
especially if the tobacco is Springbok. I speak here from
experience, because one of my dad's friends, Irving Brodie,
from the house diagonally behind ours, smokes a pipe with
Springbok tobacco. Ugh! As soon as he walks in the house I

can smell it on him, even before he takes out his black pipe and his yellow and white pouch of Springbok tobacco.

I don't know how he manages to be director of an advertising agency. The only thing he could persuade me to do would be to keep a healthy distance between him and me. But still he keeps on trying to persuade non-whites to buy washing-up liquid, even though they've managed for years without some polluting yellow chemical in a squeezy bottle; and still he tries to persuade them to use toothpaste even though some of their teeth, especially the African's teeth, are far whiter and healthier than Irving Brodie's teeth which are stained yellow from tobacco.

Really, when those two get together to play chess, if possible, you should try and spend the day in Oudtshoorn. Because the room gets all murky with cigar smoke and pipe smoke and openings and endgames, and before long they are cursing each other and blaming each other for the wrong moves they made. Yet, at the end of a session, they always arrange to play again.

'That was a good game,' Irving says, 'especially the endgame.'

'No, the endgame was spoiled when you knocked over your pipe and interrupted my concentration,' my dad says. 'But next time I'll definitely beat you. It's my turn to play white.'

My ma used to get mad at them for making so much mess on the carpet and the furniture, but the next morning it was Dolly who would have to clean it all up with the vacuum cleaner.

'What for are these ashtrays?' Dolly would complain. 'They think a ashtray is a ornament!'

You know what those two guys reminded me of? Of the story of how Table Mountain got its cloth.

I first heard that story when I was kid. My ma was a great storyteller: every night she would tell me a different story. I don't know where my ma got all those ideas from; I

84

suppose they just sprung up in her brain like a hot spring, but some of the stories she got from books. One of my favourites was how Table Mountain got its tablecloth.

That tablecloth must definitely be one of the seven natural wonders of the world. Every so often it gets laid there, a beautiful white cloth of clouds sitting on the flat tabletop, just as if guests were expected. The best view of it, I think, is from Bloubergstrand, looking across the bay. Even if I live to be 100 and move to the Kalahari Desert, I'll never forget that image. It's burned into my soul just like they brand cattle with a number in the movies. Also I was born halfway up the lower slopes of Table Mountain, in the Hope Nursing Home, so the first air I ever breathed was the air around that mountain.

The story of the tablecloth concerns the retired pirate, Ort van Hunks, who settled in Cape Town at the time when it was still a halfway-house on the shipping route to India. There had been nothing halfway about his pirating; he was stinking rich, so he could afford a nice farm with many strong slaves to work it for him.

His only trouble was his fat, nagging wife, who complained to him regularly that his tobacco was falling to the floor and making burnmarks on her lovely furniture. So Van Hunks had to get away from her every so often, and where he went was to this ridge between Table Mountain and Devil's Peak. There he sat smoking his clay pipe without disturbance, looking down on the fairest Cape in all the world, watching the old-fashioned sailing ships resting in the harbour.

But one time as he sat there, he was disturbed by this sudden, irritating voice.

'Morning meneer! You don't mind if I join you, do you?' a little man said, doffing his hat.

'Who the hell are you?' Van Hunks asked.

'Very well put,' the intruder said, turning around to

show his backside where his pointed tail protruded from a carefully tailored slit in his pantaloons.

'You're sitting on my peak,' he said, pointing to the Devil's Peak behind them, 'so I thought I'd come and join you.'

'The Devil, hey?' Van Hunks said, quite impressed. 'I thought I'd got away from the Devil by coming up here.'

The little man pulled out of his coat pocket a heavy iron pipe.

'You don't mind if I load up, do you?'

'Be my guest,' Van Hunks said, handing over his large pouch of tobacco.

The two men sat and smoked amicably, until Van Hunks produced his dice.

'Feel like a game?' he asked the Devil.

'What could be better?' the Devil answered. 'Where's your money?'

Van Hunks fancied he could beat the Devil at any game, no matter what stakes they played for. He opened his bag of loot on to the rock. This loot was still left over from his pirating days. There were gold coins and silver goblets and diamond rings, some still with fingers in them.

'Is that all you've got?' the Devil asked.

'I wasn't expecting you,' Van Hunks answered.

'Oh, alright then, I'll give you credit on your soul, if necessary.'

'That won't be necessary,' Van Hunks thought to himself, knowing full well that his dice were loaded and that he could not lose.

So they started playing, and they smoked as they played, and as they played they smoked, and the more they played, the more they smoked, and the more they smoked, the more they played, until the smoke was so dense, it became difficult to see the dice. They knocked out their pipes, refilled with tobacco, and began again, smoking and playing, playing and smoking.

This is the part of the story that I get reminded of when I see my dad and Irving Brodie playing chess. The only difference is that I've never noticed either of them having a tail.

Anyhow, while they were playing, a fierce south-easterly wind blew up, and as well as giving the sailing ships in the harbour a rough time, it also blew the white smoke across the flat top of Table Mountain.

The dice game continued, with the pipes being lit again and again, until the billowing cloud completely shrouded Table Mountain.

Finally, Van Hunks excused himself.

'I must go now, otherwise that wife of mine will give me a worse hell than you could ever imagine.'

He stood up, gathering his winnings, and his pipe and tobacco.

The Devil also stood up; his tail no longer protruded from his pantaloons as it had been handed over to pay his debt.

'You must come play again,' the Devil said, 'so that I can win back my tail and also your soul.'

'Not until next summer,' Van Hunks said. 'I suffer terribly from the arthritis. I never come up here in winter.'

And so it is, year after year, whenever Van Hunks and the Devil gamble with each other that the thick cloth of smoke from their pipes covers Table Mountain.

Well, that's the story as my ma told it, and I always used to think it was a good story when I was kid. But it was the Brodies' garden boy, Amos, who showed me that there are at least two sides to every story.

Amos has worked in the garden of that house ever since I can remember. First he worked for the Rudniks until Mrs Rudnik died. When the Brodies took over, they asked Amos to stay on, because he was so reliable and had looked after the place so well.

The Brodies had no children, or maybe they did, but they were all grown up. So why they wanted such a big place, I'll never know. They entertained a lot, and often seemed to have people staying with them, but their sparkling swimming pool and tennis court were hardly ever used.

If it wasn't for Dolly, I would never have found out this thing about Amos that really shocked me. Dolly knows everything that goes on in the neighbourhood. She and her friends can gossip for hours about what's going on in each of the houses, with the masters and the madams, and what's going on with the servants, and with the garden boys, and even, I'm sure, what's going on with the dogs and the cats. In fact she gossiped so much that my dad once asked her if anyone paid her for bits of gossip.

'No, Master,' she said.

'Well, I don't see why I should pay you either for gossiping.'

That cut down her gossiping for a while, but not for ever.

Anyway, she certainly knew what was going on with Amos, because she had this thing going with him, even though he had lots of Xhosa blood in him, I think, and she was mostly coloured. She used to spend a lot of her off-time with him even though she had another boyfriend, Floyd, who pestered her constantly to marry him. In fact, she had been strolling with Floyd near Kirstenbosch Gardens, she said, when she had found the handbag belonging to Mrs Kraichik, and it had been on his advice that Dolly had returned the handbag to its owner, even though she admitted the jewels were so tempting.

'You take those and you'll get married to a jail,' Floyd had warned her.

My young brother, Ivan, and me always used to have this joke about Amos.

'Knock, knock!'
'Who's there?'
'Amos.'
'Amos who?'
'A mosquito.'

I don't suppose it was at all funny really, but it used to make Ivan laugh, so forever in our heads Amos became Amosquito.

'I saw Dolly holding hands with Amosquito,' I would say and Ivan's face would light up.

'Amosquito likes her, doesn't he?' Ivan would say.

'Yes, but Dolly's boyfriend, Floyd, doesn't like Amosquito,' I would say.

'Do you think Dolly will marry Floyd or Amosquito?' Ivan would say, cracking up with laughter.

So it came as quite a shock to me one day when Dolly let slip that Amos had just passed his matric. Passed his matric? God, I thought, I didn't know that Amosquito could pass even Standard 2!

'But he hasn't been going to school, Dolly,' I said.

'Night school,' she said. 'He has been going to night school for years and years.'

'Now he can get a good job and you two can get married.'

Dolly smiled coyly and looked at the ground.

'First he's going to learn correspondence,' she said.

The next time I was in the garden near the Brodies' loquat tree that used to hang over into our garden, I watched Amos digging the vegetable garden.

He looked up at me and caught me watching him.

'Dolly says you passed matric,' I said to him. 'Congratulations!'

'Thank you, Basil,' he said. I never even knew that he knew my name.

'Dolly says that maybe you will do a correspondence course.'

'No, I'm not so sure. It took me so long to do matric in my off-time. Maybe I will do articles. I want to be a lawyer one day, if I don't get too old.'

I looked at Amos. I suppose he was getting on, but he still wore his old brown velskoen shoes with the laces untied, the same way he'd worn them ever since I could remember.

It struck me that you could never have guessed from someone's shoes what the person who was wearing them was really like.

'You're not too old to be a lawyer,' I said.

'I hope not,' he said. 'Our people have a great need for lawyers. What are you going to study when you leave school?'

'Journalism,' I said.

'Well, it's a good job as long as you tell the bitter truth, hey! You mustn't add a sugar coating to what's going in this country.'

From that time on, I always tried to chat to Amos over the fence. He never stopped his weeding or digging while I was talking, but he seemed to enjoy my conversation and I enjoyed his, at least until the day he told me his opinion of the Van Hunks story.

It came up because he was talking about how he had been a gardener in white people's gardens for so many years.

'It's okay if it's your own garden,' he said. 'But working this hard for someone else is completely stupid. Especially for the rubbish wage *he* pays me.'

He pointed derisively towards Mr Brodie's house.

'Don't you get paid well?'

'Look at these grounds. I know every corner of grass here, and everything growing in it, and I've done all the work here, and *he* doesn't ever step outside here to even look at his own property.'

'I know what you mean,' I said. 'It's not right.'

I was proud that I could talk so easily with a non-white and vice versa, that he could talk so easily with me. Especially about his opinions of white people.

'This is such a beautiful place, man,' he said, looking up at the mountain behind him. 'This should be shared for all people.'

'I agree with you,' I said. 'But there's a lot of white people who think they own all this.'

Amos stopped for a rare instant.

'How can anyone *own* mountains or land or sky?' he said.

I didn't answer. I looked where he was pointing.

'See those clouds,' he said. 'They will soon lay the tablecloth up there. Don't you think that's one of the seven wonders of the world?'

'Ja,' I said. 'Old Van Hunks must be having a good smoke up there with the Devil.'

Amos looked at me like I was mad.

'I thought you knew better, Basil.'

'Knew what?'

'That Van Hunks story is a load of bulldust! You want to be a journalist, man – can't you see that it's a white man's story? They tell it to each other to make it seem that even the tablecloth on Table Mountain was made by a white man. And what's more, a corrupt white man who kept slaves to do his labour and who cheated when he played dice. That tablecloth, don't you know, used to blow up on that mountain top long before any white man ever arrived in the Cape in his little boats. It has been there since that mountain was born! Only a white man could come up with this idea that the tablecloth is only 300 years old. And only a white man would believe such nonsense. I didn't expect *you* to believe it. It's a bad story anyway, because how long do you think the white man can cheat the Devil without losing his soul?'

I was taken back by the force of his outburst. Didn't he realize that I had the power, if I wanted, to go and tell Mr Brodie everything? I could repeat Amos's words about rubbish wages and I'm sure Mr Brodie wouldn't have hesitated to fire Amos on the spot.

On the other hand, Amos obviously had a good point.

'I don't *believe* that story, Amos. I've never thought about it the way you have. But you're right. It is a white man's story. I was just referring to it as a stupid story that I was told when I was a kid.'

91

'Ja, well, Basil, nothing's as simple as it looks.'

I don't know who was more disappointed, Dolly or me, when Amos suddenly left his job. I suppose Dolly must have been, because her hopes of freedom vanished into thin air like a magician's trick.

Amos disappeared without saying a word to anyone. I supposed he didn't want to have an upsetting farewell scene with Dolly.

A few days afterwards, she heard that there had been one almighty argument between Mr Brodie and Amos.

'That man is terrible!' Dolly said to me. 'He found one of Amos's books and he said he would call the police if Amos didn't leave straight away.'

'Why?' I asked. 'What's so wrong about a book?'

The incident was confirmed by my ma when she bumped into Mr Brodie one day at the hypermarket.

'That's what comes of being liberal with these people!' Mr Brodie had said to her. 'It's not worth it. You give them a baby finger and they want the whole hand. Did you know that boy got his matric? A garden boy with matric! Have you ever heard of anything so ridiculous? And then he gets so big for his boots, he even reads his books while he's supposed to be working.'

Since that time, Dolly has been waiting three years for a word or something from Amos. I think she still believes that he will call for her one day like a prince in shining armour and ask her to marry him.

'Then I will start my new life,' she says.

But Amos never called for her. She heard a rumour once, though, through a cousin of a friend of hers who works in Oranjezicht, that Amos was working in the garden there for another white family.

'Maybe he will always be a gardener,' I said.

'No way,' she said. 'Not Amos. He has a ambition and he will do it, for sure.'

A few months later, she told me that she had heard from

92

her brother that he knew a man who had been arrested during a protest march, and that he was being defended in the court-case by a new lawyer who looked like a Xhosa. And the thing that convinced her the lawyer was Amos, was that although he had shiny new black patent leather shoes, he walked about with the laces untied.

As it turned out, Dolly afterwards found it very useful to personally know of a lawyer. That was the time when Floyd was arrested and taken to court for stealing ladies' handbags.

The future is ours

It's strange that a government should take such an interest in a person's body.

I mean when Hester Conradie from across the road let the boys look at her naked, she charged us one rand a go. But I don't think the government ever paid her a rand when they called her into their offices one day to check if she was coloured or not.

It is true that Hester's skin was a lot darker than either of her two young brothers', and it was also darker than either her father's or her mother's. But so what? My skin is very different from my young brother's: I'm fair and go red whenever I sunbathe, but my brother goes a nice brown and stays like that the whole summer. And what about my ma? Even my dad jokes that she doesn't look European when she's tanned. But the government never came and took her to their Race Classification Offices for an examination.

I don't honestly know how those government inspectors (or whoever they were) decided. But the half moons on her fingernails must have been more like a new moon, or the thickness of her lips must have been a millimetre over the limit for whites, or her hair must have had one or two crinkles too many in it. I don't know. Maybe they stuck a pencil in her hair like Mr Getz said, and it stuck so hard she couldn't shake it out. But whatever it was, she went to that office a white person and came back coloured.

To me she looked identical – no browner – just the same old sexy Hester that I'd let my eyes roam over a few years back.

I hadn't spoken all that much to her in those years between paying my rand and her being turned into a coloured. But you would have had to be blind not to notice how rounded and pretty she was. Between us we just managed the odd embarrassed sort of conversation, you know: 'Hi, there, how's thing's going?' 'Okay, and you?' But on the other hand, my dreams were full of her. Every time those desires grew in my brain and in other places too, it was Hester's shape that came to mind. And she had the sort of shape that filled most of the space in a bloke's mind.

I used to dream that Hester was my girlfriend for the night and that she liked me enough to let me do anything and everything, and vice versa, of course, too. Every time I needed the cuddles of a dreamgirl, it was always Hester. She was like a ghost that inhabited my bedroom. And not only my bedroom. Sometimes when I went out with other girls, suddenly the Hester ghost would enter my mind and make a comparison between herself and the female I was with, and often the female in question came off second best.

Hester's reclassification made no odds to my fantasies either. For some mad reason, difficult to fathom, it was the opposite. I couldn't get her out of my mind after that. I decided that next time I saw her, I would definitely try to get to know her a lot better.

But the next time was a long time coming. Mr and Mrs Conradie must have confined her indoors until they came to their decisions about what to do under the changed circumstances.

Can you imagine the shock that her parents got when they were informed about Hester now being a coloured?

The people in our neighbourhood spoke about nothing else.

Suddenly her parents had to believe that somewhere lurking in their chromosomes was a coloured gene – maybe an African, or a Malay, or even a Hottentot gene! I thought the arguments between my ma and dad were bad, but can you imagine Mr and Mrs Conradie arguing about who owned the scandalous gene?

Mr Getz had another theory altogether. He had always had suspicions that the Conradies were coloured, even though on the pale side. But his new idea was that Hester's father was a black man. Can you work that out? It took me a while. That's right, man, he must have come to the conclusion that Mrs Conradie had an affair with a black man! How he knew I just don't know! But maybe he just had a good eye for those sorts of things.

Apart from the issue of genes and illicit love affairs, it put the Conradies in a terrible position. Because now that one of their children was declared non-white, there was a certain pressure on them to leave the area altogether.

But they resisted, even though a meeting of neighbourhood residents was organized for those who were determined to hound them out of the area. Mr and Mrs Conradie insisted that their family had lived on that plot for 111 years and they weren't about to leave because of a stupid government reclassification of their daughter's skin.

A hundred and eleven years of residence sounded like a good long stay to me, and a good enough reason not to move. After all, it was about 102 years longer than the Getz's or our family had lived in that area.

However, one day a few bricks were found in the Conradie's backyard, just near to where their two young boys used to play. Those bricks hadn't been there the day before and I guess the Conradies thought that they were unidentified flying objects, because of the way they came flying over the high hedge, and because the white people

who threw them ran away so fast they were never identified.

Those bricks must have tipped the balance in helping the
Conradies to make a decision. Those bricks, plus the fact
that the boarding school where Hester had been a pupil for
the past four years *invited* her to leave, because it was an all-
white school.

It was decided that Hester would board with a family in
Grassy Park and continue her education at the Grootvlei
High School for coloureds.

So my intention of getting to know her better came to
nothing for the meanwhile.

She hardly ever stepped inside her parents' house after
that. Once or twice during the school holidays she used to
come to visit them, but only for a morning or an afternoon.
She didn't stay long and I always missed her coming out.

So I decided to keep careful watch and pretend to
accidentally bump into her as she came out of her drive-
way.

Eventually it happened. But as soon as I was face to face
with her, I could feel myself going a tomato red colour,
because the thought occurred to me that maybe she somehow knew about my fantasies of her. I could have saved
myself the embarrassment, though, because it was the
furthest thought from her mind.

'How's your new school, Hester?'

She looked at me in a way that made me feel terrible, as if
I had been the one who had reclassified her non-white.

'What do you care about those schools?'

I struggled in my head for something real to say.

'Hester, I'm sorry what happened to you.'

She hardly looked at me, but continued walking up
towards the bus stop. I walked a pace behind her.

'Please, Hester, why don't you talk to me?'

'Because you're part of the oppressive system.'

'I don't want to be,' I said.

'But if you do nothing, then that's what you are. You just take all the privileges and you don't even let coloured people live like human beings. You relocate them, and give them gutter education, and deprive them of a real vote, and . . .'

I could see that she had been learning a lot in her new school.

'. . . you don't let them share in the running of their own lives.'

'That's true,' I said. 'But aren't things changing?'

'Come to my school for a few days and you'll find out.'

'What do you mean?'

'It's not things that are changing,' she said. 'It's people that change. People like me and all the other coloureds at my school and throughout the Cape. We're all changing. You whites used to think you were superior to us, but that was all lies. We're sick of this white propaganda you give us. From now on we're equals whether you like it or lump it. From next week we're boycotting the school and we're demanding our rights as human beings. You just watch what's going to happen in the next few weeks. You whites will never change, unless we change you.'

I could see the bus coming down the hill. I wanted to tell Hester that I had changed already, at least a little, and couldn't she give me a bit of chance to change more? I wanted to say something to her that would show her I was not only on her side, but that I liked her a lot and thought of her all the time. I didn't care what the government called her; to me she was Hester.

But the bus came and I was as dumb as the weeds growing on the pavement by the bus stop and I never said anything to her. She got on that bus without looking back at me and holding her head high.

In the following weeks I saw scenes from those boycotts on TV. I specially watched, though it was truly horrible: what started off as peaceful protest by hundreds of school-

kids just like Hester, always ended up with the arrival of
the security forces in their hippo vehicles and anti-riot gear.
Then the battles began, the kids hurling bottles and stones
at the forces, putting up barricades and setting fire to school
buildings, while the police, and sometimes even armed
soldiers, roared towards them, lobbing canisters of teargas
into the crowds. Schoolkids tried to resist by tying wet
handkerchiefs around their mouths and noses, but many of
them collapsed or were beaten with sjamboks made from
rhinoceros hide or quirts made of plastic. And many of
them were arrested.

I never actually saw Hester on TV, nor her school even –
it was always other kids in other schools – yet every day I
had dreams of her, protesting for her rights, with a wet
handkerchief around her face, or at the receiving end of
those vicious sjamboks and quirts. These dreams were so
excruciating to me, it spoiled all the fun I used to have of
imagining her cuddling with me.

Sometimes I awoke at night screaming and gasping for
breath as if it was me caught in teargas or the smoke from
burning tyres and buildings. The smoke or gas was choking
me as if there was a lump of something stuck in my throat.
My awakening always took a few seconds, before I realized
that I was as comfortable in my white bed as I could
possibly wish to be, with all the luxuries of my life spread
around me and at my disposal. But feeling my own
comfortableness never lulled me back into sleep. Somehow
it screwed me up inside. It drove me mad worrying about
her. I wished the boycott would soon be over.

It was difficult for me to talk to anyone about my
sleeplessness. The guys at my school would have thought it
was weird that I was so troubled by the disturbances at a
coloured school. I'm not saying there weren't some guys
who sympathized with the coloureds. Rael Chandler, for
example – I know for a fact that he was in favour of mixed

education. But still I wasn't able to tell him something so personal.

'You're getting rings under your eyes, Basil,' my ma said one morning before school. 'You go to sleep too late. You're still a growing boy.'

'Yes, Ma, I know.'

'Are you getting enough exercise?'

'Yes, Ma, you know I do.'

'I wonder if you're short of vitamins.'

'Come off it, Ma!'

'But a boy your age shouldn't have rings under your eyes. You look like you've been in the wars.'

It's not me who's in the wars, Ma, I wanted to say. I'm sure she would have understood, because in her job she's dealt with the problems of coloureds for so long. But would she have understood that I was concerned about one particular coloured, and a coloured girl, what's more?

Then one late afternoon, I noticed two police cars driving into the Conradie's place. I kept watch through the venetian blinds in our lounge and saw them drive off at about six-thirty. I thought, oh no, Hester's in trouble! She's been arrested or something. Maybe they're going to put her in prison for agitating. I stayed up most of the night worrying.

The next morning through the venetian blinds I saw another police car pull in to the Conradie's drive, and by mid-afternoon a couple of newspaperman were congregating outside their property. One of them had a camera and was taking pictures of the surrounding hedge. However, when he attempted to walk up their long gravel drive, somebody must have shouted at him to shove off, because he came scuttling back down the drive.

It had only been a couple of years since the last time the newspapermen had come round, but then it was in connection with Hester's reclassification. One newspaperman at that time even had the cheek to knock on our door to ask if we had any information to add to the scandal.

'I wonder if you could tell me whether the Conradies mostly have white or coloured friends?' he had asked.

My dad told the bloke that his questions were unwelcome, but the bloke persisted and my dad shut the door in his face; he wasn't at all keen on journalists.

It probably wasn't the same newspaperman who I could see standing there now two years later, photographing a carful of young people dressed in green uniforms driven by a smartly dressed coloured lady. It arrived midway through the morning and turned slowly into the drive. Maybe Hester's ill or hurt, I thought, and her schoolfriends have come to visit her. But why all the police?

By lunchtime I couldn't stand the suspense any longer. I went outside and approached the man with the camera who was standing by the Conradie's hedge.

'What's going on?' I asked.

'Haven't you heard?' he answered.

'Heard what?'

'About the Conradie's daughter.'

My heart started palpitating.

'What about her?'

'She's dead. Outside her school.'

Dead? The word hit me somewhere deep. A red curtain came over my eyes and I felt the world swirling around giddily. I tried to keep standing upright, but the world wanted to fade away. How could she be dead? Nobody so young and lovely could be dead! The world wouldn't make any sense if she was dead. It would just be a world of wasted energy. A place for madmen. A place where things disintegrate in front of your own eyes, where nothing keeps its shape long enough for a person to figure it out. Everyone would be walking around in a state of blind fear.

'Are you alright?'

The man put out a hand towards me, but I shrugged it off. His gesture was meaningless, didn't he know? I wanted to run away. But where? There was no hiding place in the world where Hester's death wasn't known, no hiding place which hadn't been contaminated by fear.

'The official story is that she tripped over a stone when she was running away from the teargas . . .'

I heard the words, though I couldn't understand what he was trying to tell me. What the hell is an official story? Hester was dead. Not the girl in my dreams – no, the real flesh and blood Hester!

'. . . but if she tripped, how did she manage to crush the top of her skull, that's what I want to know.'

The man's voice droned on, but his words weren't joined together properly with the glue of meaning.

Oh, Hester! Why didn't I ever get really near to you? Why did you only live in my dreams? I should have done something, I know I should. I should have reached out to you.

I thought I could hear singing in the distance. Who could be singing? There were many voices in harmony and the singing was getting louder. How could anyone be singing if Hester truly was dead?

The car driven by the coloured lady emerged from the Conradie's drive. The young people in their green uniforms were singing a song whose words I couldn't make out. But they held their fists out of the car windows and some of them shouted 'Viva!' and 'Amandla!' as they drove past the photographers and one of them held out a placard on which was written in large black letters: 'The future is ours!'

You were right, Hester, we whites will never change unless you change us. I should have had the guts to stand by you, to take your side against the world. Now it's too late. You had guts, Hester, but me? I'm a nothing. I'm hollowed out. My insides are just one screaming ball of fear.

As the car drove up the road and disappeared around the corner, I knew I wanted to be one of those people with a claim on the future, singing and shouting out freedom slogans, but I also knew that I would never be one of them. The fear inside me was so great, it threatened to drown my present life, never mind my future.

Oh, Hester! What really happened to you?

For the second time in a matter of years, Hester's body was suddenly of great interest to the government. On this occasion, though, it was for their doctors to establish the cause of death of the person they had reclassified as coloured.

Stolen fire

Dewie Getz's father was in the construction business, so it wasn't surprising that his own house should be a model of what his company could construct. My dad said it was such a good model that no wonder the business was going bankrupt.

It was the only double storey on our road, though of course, the house with the loquat tree diagonally behind us was also double storey. But that wasn't on our road, and it wasn't constructed by the Getz Building Company, so it didn't look anything like a terrarium.

The Getz house was centred around this internal garden, which you could see from most rooms through enormous glass windows. The internal garden had a glass pyramid of a roof, so that the rubber trees which grew in there were certainly the tallest in Africa.

The outside of the house was also mainly glass – no iron burglar bars or wires in sight because Mr Getz had installed the latest laser alarm system or something. From the house there were wide glass doors leading to the proper garden, which was only a third of an acre but was landscaped with interesting hills and rockeries. My dad couldn't see the point of making artificial hills in your garden, when Table Mountain itself was just at the bottom of the road with all its natural rockeries stretching up 1,000 metres into the sky.

The Getz residence was surrounded by a three metre

high brick wall topped by broken glass set in cement. This not only protected them from burglars, but kept what went on at the Getz's well out of sight. Actually you could hardly see that wall from the Getz's house, because of the different bushes and creepers which grew in front of it, giving the impression that you were in a glasshouse surrounded by a natural jungle. But one of those creepers grew granadillas, and I must say, they were massively tasty.

The stairs from downstairs to up were open slats of wood supported from the roof by iron bars. Once you were upstairs, you could look down from every room through the glass pyramid over the indoor garden. It was very modern when it was built, my dad said, but that style is now out of date, though how he knew so much about its style I don't know, because I don't ever remember him going inside their house.

But though my dad had strong opinions about the Getz's house, he had much stronger opinions about Mr Getz's terrible temper. He was always on about how a bull shouldn't live in a china shop, and especially not a wild Cape Buffalo, and how people who throw stones shouldn't live in glass houses.

I must say, the one time I slept over at Dewie's place, I began to see what my dad was on about. His voice, when he spoke to his wife and to his children and to their coloured servant Caroline, was like the roar of a Cape Buffalo, though I'm not sure if a Cape Buffalo roars, maybe it just bellows. But the man was certainly as big as a buffalo – and his temper flared up like a buffalo's horns at the smallest thing.

Poor Mrs Getz wasn't a big lady. She was thin like Dewie's sister Nolene, and when Mr Getz roared at her, her body shook like a leaf.

'Haven't I told you that the outside door must be kept locked?' he screamed at her. 'Otherwise Caroline will have half the coloureds in Cape Town coming to visit her! And you must know what these coloureds are like. They would steal the shirt from their own child.'

There was something else about Mr Getz that was a bit odd, which I discovered at the evening meal. That night they ate fish, kingklip or something, but Mr Getz wasn't just satisfied with the flesh. He also ate the fish's eyes. I must admit, I couldn't look at him slicing them, and it put me right off my food.

He also offended me when he spoke about my father.

'And how's your father finding the furniture trade? Is he making lots of money?'

'What should the boy know about his father's business?' Mrs Getz warbled.

'Because Kushentochus is a big talker,' Mr Getz answered quietly aside, thinking I wouldn't hear him twist our surname to mean 'kiss my arse.'

'Our name is Kushenovitz,' I mumbled sullenly.

In the middle of the night I woke up and could hear the roaring. I went to the toilet and looking down through the glass pyramid I could see Mr Getz screaming at his wife and I'm sure he was hitting her as well – but it was difficult to see through all that glass. I didn't tell my dad about that beating, because I didn't want him to get a bad opinion of my best friend's dad.

At breakfast next morning, you would have thought everyone had a peaceful night. But I was still having trouble eating, because of this mush on toast that was put on my plate. Out of politeness I tasted it, but it made me feel like vomiting. All the Getz's gobbled theirs down.

'Don't you like sheep's brains?' Mr Getz asked me.

Of course, I tried to avoid ever sleeping there again, but Dewie and me were always good friends, right up to matric. We had gone to the same primary school, and we stayed friends right through high school, even though his dad sent him to a posh school in Rondebosch.

We argued a lot, because we were so different – that was

just part of being friends. But last year our friendship hit the rocks.

It was when Nev came to visit us.

Nev's dad, Barney, was an old friend of my dad's who lived in Joburg. For many years he had threatened to come down and visit us, and finally he did – by bike. I'm not kidding, him and Nev, who was nearly eighteen, one year older than I was, cycled all the way down from Joeys to Cape Town.

They turned up by surprise, what's more, without a word's warning. There they were on our stoep in all their cycling gear and leaning against their two touring bikes. It had taken them three weeks to do it but they looked proud as hell that they had accomplished it.

They stayed two weeks before going back to Joburg – by train, this time, and who could blame them? It's one thing cruising downhill from Joburg to Cape town, but who wants to pedal uphill all the way to the Highveld? Anyway, who in their right mind would want to ride through the dusty Karroo twice?

Nev had already been out of school one year, and having cycled all the way from Joburg to Cape Town, plus being from the City of Gold, he naturally thought highly of himself.

The first night he arrived, he arranged for us to walk up the back of Table Mountain the next day. He didn't even have to check it out with his dad.

My dad suggested the route Jan Smuts used to walk in the old days. It was a great day for mountain climbing; the only problem was that Dewie and me had trouble keeping up with Nev, even though he carried the heaviest rucksack. We watched his powerful calf muscles for hour upon hour as he hiked up the slope.

At one point on the route, a snake was basking on the path. When I saw that deadly cobra, I suddenly realized what a fine day it was to rather go to the beach, but Nev said

I shouldn't be so scared of a harmless grass snake. He threw a stick at it, and it slithered off into the bush.

By the time we reached the summit, the sight of Nev's calf muscles were beginning to grate Dewie. He had been irritable all the way and I knew he would soon be in a fury.

'This is a bladdy waste of time!' he said.

'But look at the view!' I said, sitting and loosening my boots.

'I'm going to explore this area,' Nev said. 'Any of you okes coming?'

Dewie scowled, so I said to Nev we'd make our own way down, in our own time.

When we reached home, Dewie was angry as hell. Especially when we found that Nev had already been back nearly an hour.

'Listen,' Dewie said to me, 'don't ask me along any more if your Joburg pal is with you, okay?'

I think Dewie was going through a rough time at home. At least that's what my dad implied. He said he'd heard that the Getz's were involved in a law suit, and he was only surprised that the matter hadn't reached the back page of the Sunday papers.

But Nev persuaded Dewie and me to come out with him one more time. Nev managed to borrow my mom's car. Now how he did that, I don't know, because I'm still sure he wasn't eighteen yet. But, in any event, he got the use of the Renault. Normally my dad wouldn't let anyone borrow either of our cars, not even if God himself wanted to drive to Cape Point to check on the join between the Atlantic and the Indian Oceans.

Nev drove via de Waal's Drive into the city, as if he had lived in Cape Town all his life. Not one wrong turn. He cruised along the city centre whistling at chicks and hooting here and there. Finally, he stopped at a flower market.

He approached one flower seller after another. I never knew the guy was so interested in flowers. Eventually he seemed to find the kind he was looking for. This coloured man was laughing with Nev like they had known each other since the Garden of Eden.

Finally Nev pulled out a few notes and paid the flower seller. But the coloured man didn't start wrapping a bunch of dahlias or a bunch of roses. No, the parcel he wrapped was only as long as a finger.

'We're on our way!' Nev said, revving up the Renault, like he was on Killarney racetrack. He was so confident, wearing these dark glasses, even though by now the sun had already set.

He drove out of the city centre and made his way into the dingy streets somewhere behind Woodstock. I had never been in those parts before and I'm sure my dad would have burst a blood vessel knowing we were in such a disreputable part of town. Of course, if Dewie's dad had known, life wouldn't have been worth living, because not only were these streets disreputable, but the woman parading herself on the pavement wasn't even white.

She gave us her best smile as we climbed out of the car.

'Hey, Mr Glasses,' she said, (to Nev, of course, who else?) 'I give you a special discount.'

'Not now, baby,' Nev said.

'What about you guys?' she said to Dewie and me. 'You want a goose?'

Dewie gave me this look which said everything.

'Let's get out of here!' he whispered to me.

'Come on, man,' I said. 'Let's see what Nev's up to.'

We walked round the back of these shops and I could hear a drumbeat and some music coming from an upstairs window.

Nev walked straight towards this one door as if he knew it well, turned the handle and went in just as if he lived there.

There were a few coloured people milling around the

kitchen, but Nev found the stairs and up he went, Dewie and me following like two of his apostles.

The source of the music was a live band centred around this out of tune piano – I think the band was mostly coloureds – and the room was full of people. Some were sitting at this long table in the one room, drinking and smoking. Others were standing in groups chatting. Still others were dancing cheek to cheek.

Now if it had surprised Dewie that the house was full of coloureds, it was even more surprising to him that there were whites among them. White men and white women. It was mindboggling. Even I felt a queasiness in my stomach, but Dewie looked like he had been eating too much sheep's brains. I'm telling you, he was frightened. Frightened of being caught in this place or frightened of catching something in this place – I don't know what he was frightened of, but he wanted to get the hell out.

'This is a den of vice,' he said.

Nev mingled freely – no problem. Within a few minutes he had rolled a cigarette, and he was puffing away and chatting to people of all colours.

Then to my astonishment he passed me the cigarette.

'Here have a drag, man. It will make you feel better.'

I had never smoked in my life, so I'm not quite sure why I agreed. Probably because this was even more of an adventure than following in Jan Smuts's footsteps up the backside of Table Mountain.

I took a few puffs, coughed a bit, took a few more, and then passed it on to Dewie, who was an experienced smoker. But I think he smoked Rembrandt van Rijn, and this thing I passed him didn't look anything like Rembrandt van Rijn. Still he was desperate and took a few drags.

Now I must admit that when I first walked into that house, it looked really dingy and the people in it looked like down and outs of the worst kind. But suddenly I noticed that the music the band was playing had improved a lot. I didn't know why I had first thought that the piano was out of tune. On the contrary, the notes were tinkling in a most heavenly combination, and the chords on the guitar sounded like they were on my own nervestrings being plucked. What's more, the sound of the muted trumpet seemed to carry me down a long passageway of memory to where my ma was falling down in our dining room. Yes, she was very fat at the time – fat belly. That's right, she was pregnant. And my dad came running in and picked her up and helped her to the sofa.

'Ag, shame, doesn't he look so sad,' this coloured lady was saying to me. 'You mustn't be so sad. Maybe it will never happen.'

She pulled out a tissue and wiped my eyes. I couldn't understand why – maybe she thought I had been crying.

I looked up at her. Her eyes were so beautiful. They were eyes from another planet, so understanding, so compassionate. Yes, the pregnancy miscarried, now I remember. And Ivan and me never had another brother or sister.

The lady held my hand and introduced me to her boyfriend.

'Here, Billy, you cheer up this lightie.'

I didn't want the lady to leave. But Billy was talking to me and I watched his mouth moving.

'Come sit down, man, and tell me your worries.'

'I haven't got worries,' I said, but I sat down at this table anyway.

There was a candle burning in front of me. Its flame was burning so perfectly, I couldn't believe it. More perfectly than any other candle I had ever seen. How that flame flickered – with its blue and orange and red layers! The more I watched, the more I couldn't understand what fire even was. No wonder in my encyclopaedia it said that fire had originally been stolen from the gods. It was like watching a private show of the gods, and I felt so lucky to be invited.

'This is your first time, hey?' Billy said to me.

I said yes, but I didn't know which first time he meant, unless he also could see the miracle of that burning flame.

'You must just let it all happen,' Billy said.

I heard his words and I tried to let it all happen, but I wasn't sure what I was letting happen.

'You whites are so opgeboggered. Screwed up, hey, like nobody's business. You must relax and not be so tight up your arse.'

I heard his words and I tried to relax the muscles he was referring to. It felt better, I must say.

'One day it will all be different, hey?' he said. 'We won't hide in little rooms, but we'll come out in the sunshine and dance, hey?'

Yes, I wanted to do that very much. I wanted Billy to show me the sunshine and the dancing.

'That's better,' he said. 'You're smiling a bit. Your cheek won't crack, you know.'

The rolled-up cigarette came Billy's way again. He cupped his hands and took a deep breath. Then another, and another.

I put out my hands to take it from him, but he passed it to someone on the other side.

'No, my brother,' he said in Afrikaans. 'You don't need more.'

I looked up at Billy. Was he my brother like he said? Ag, no, it couldn't be. This man was coloured. But so what? He was looking after me like a brother does.

'Billy, does he feel better?'

It was the coloured lady again asking if I was feeling better.

'I've never felt better, honestly,' I said.

'Hey, Cherry, do you feel like a dance?' she asked.

'Who me?' I said, because I must have forgotten if my name was Cherry.

'Yes, you, Cherry. Why not? Billy's okay.'

She took me in her arms and if I was ever embarrassed with people of the opposite sex, I must have also forgotten all about it, because I just danced with her slowly around the room. And towards the end of the dance, she put her cheek on mine and said 'You dance good, Cherry.'

When I sat down again, there was a face on the person next to me that I vaguely recognized.

'Who are you?' I asked.

'It's me, Dewie,' he said, grinning at me and putting his arm over my shoulder, 'your old pal, Dewie.' His eyes were glazed, but he looked happy.

'Oh it's you Dewie,' I said. 'You look so different.'

And we started giggling together. Billy and his lady sat beside us.

'Life is but a stage and we are mos the actors on it,' Billy said. 'And do you know the name of the play? I'll tell you. It's called "The Merry Days of Apartheid" – ja, ja, too true!'

'Come on, Cherry,' his lady said. This time she was talking to Billy; it must have been his name also. 'Give me a dance!'

By the time we got back home, it was three in the morning. Nev parked the Renault in the garage and he and me opened our front door with the key. He said goodnight to me and I stumbled into my bedroom. As I lay down in my clothes and all, I was sure I could hear a Cape Buffalo roaring or bellowing down the road.

My dad never said anything to me about our night out, not even when my ma found my pockets full of bottle tops and cigarette stompies. I think I must have emptied one of the ashtrays into my pocket by mistake.

When Dewie came round the next day, he had a big hangover and a black eye. I couldn't remember if he'd bumped into anything the night before, but he said he had. He blamed Nev for getting us into that situation, and for the fact that his dad had nearly murdered him when he walked in smelling of dagga.

'That was a sinful place,' Dewie said to me.

'But you had a good time, hey?' I said.

'No way, man. There shouldn't be mixing like that.'

Dewie had obviously forgotten how happy he'd been the night before, or else he was ashamed of having let himself go. But, in any event, I didn't go out with Nev again during his visit. And then he and his dad caught the train back to Joburg.

My friendship with Dewie could have survived Nev's visit. But it hit trouble after the Getz's divorce made the back page of the Sunday papers. There for everyone to read in all its gory detail was the business about Dewie's father being a violent man, who had at times beaten up the members of his own family, and for years had been having this affair with another woman. It must have been so shameful for Dewie, I think.

In the end, Nolene and her mom moved out of the glasshouse and went to live with an aunt in Aliwal North. Dewie stayed on with his dad for a few months until he went into the army to do his training. (Army training was something I hoped to avoid – by hook or by crook.)

During those months I tried to speak to him, but he was so uptight. I think maybe the worst part for him was the scandalous picture on the back page of the Sunday papers, showing Mr Getz with his arm around the other woman who was cited in the divorce case. My dad didn't even have to read the article; he could see straight away from that picture that the woman was a coloured.

Sik-sik

A hobby is a funny thing, isn't it?

I wasn't really ever interested in stamps, but everyone around thought I must be, so they gave me more and more stamps, until Phil Atterley would even have been proud of the underneath of my bed.

These stamps were kept in King Edward cigar boxes, which I got from my dad. Of course, I had stamp albums. Which stamp collector hasn't? But mine were all empty except for one page of Venezuela which I stuck in during a fit of enthusiasm one year.

Don't think my stamps were just thrown in the King Edward cigar boxes. No way. They were all in envelopes labelled by country, so that if I ever got smitten with another fit of enthusiasm to stick more in, they were all ready and waiting. I even had tweezers and sticky hinges to do the job properly.

What put me off stamp collecting was Stanley Gibbons. I mean his catalogue lists all these valuable stamps, so I started checking through mine. I thought at least some of the old Cape of Good Hope stamps that my Uncle Arthur gave me must have a decent value. But obviously anyone who ever gave me stamps must have been getting rid of their old swops or something, because nearly every one of the thousands of stamps I checked in the catalogue was worth less than fifteen cents, except for one stamp from

Russia which would have been worth four rand fifty cents if it hadn't've been torn.

No, I reckon stamps were for the birds, and even then birds have got better things to do with their time.

But one year my ma got very keen on my stamps. Since the year after my granny had her leg amputated, my ma has been involved with this organization that helps coloured physically-handicapped people. She started off by working two days a week at the Woltemade Centre, and every Thursday afternoon she and another worker visited one non-white family or another in their own house. Sometimes this meant she had to go into coloured areas or whatever, which didn't please my dad, but Ma was very dedicated.

My dad and me were very worried when she began that job if she would cope with it, or whether she would sink into a depression as soon as she came into contact with physical handicaps. But Ma was so keen; she said she had got over her depression and nothing would stop her trying to help those people.

'You might not have confidence in me,' my ma said to my dad, 'but Dr Kaplan has.'

Dr Kaplan was her psychiatrist at the time of the breakdown; it was through his therapy that my ma had recovered. And not only recovered! She was a different woman, my dad said, with a strong hint of sarcasm. He wasn't at all sure about her newfound independent way of doing things, (supported always in the background by that Dr Kaplan.)

But Ma coped well at the Centre and has since become one of their full-time care workers, and there's nothing my dad can do about that, is there?

Anyhow, when my ma first mentioned I must bring some stamps along to the centre, I reckoned it was because one of the physically-handicapped must have been interested. But I couldn't have been more wrong.

I tell you, some of those handicapped were in one hell of a state. They looked to me like they'd been caught in a plague or something. There were old blokes with withered arms and withered legs, there were others with twisted mouths who could only grunt instead of speaking and there were two people with no legs at all. But at least those two now had wheelchairs, Ma told me, because when they were first found, they were just like vegetables plonked on a board and their only way of moving was by dragging themselves with their hands.

My first thought in that place was, which of those coloureds would want to have a hobby of stamp collecting? If one of those poor souls was me, I think my main hobby would have been surviving in this world.

Anyways, eventually this lady helper turns up and I guess she must be the one interested in stamps, because my ma introduces me to her and tells her I've brought along some stamps to swop.

'Anita will be along presently,' the lady says. 'She's just buying me some chicken noodle soup.'

Well, when Anita arrived, you could have picked me up with a tweezer and stuck me to the wall with a sticky hinge! She was about my age and gorgeous! Trust my ma, hey, to trick me into meeting a girl!

I was so shy at that time though, that I only managed to swop New Zealand stamps with her and nothing else.

The following week we progressed to Australia, and by the end of the year we were freely swopping stamps from Romania and Switzerland as well.

We talked a lot together, but mainly about swops and Stanley Gibbons and values. However, we never managed to get on to that really intimate level where we could freely discuss perforations or postmarks. Anyway, after the race troubles in Cape Town, her whole family left Cape Town to go and live in Canada. For six months after that, she sent me Canadian stamps, but one time I forgot to reply and so much time passed that it didn't seem worth bothering any more.

By the time Anita left Cape Town, I was so used to going to the Woltemade Centre every week, I kept it up, and went there regularly once a week until very recently.

After a while those handicapped people didn't look so plagued to me, they just seemed like ordinary people, like you and me, but with their own problems.

They soon got used to me, and one or two of them even started collecting stamps. But mostly they liked to play cards with me for small stakes of matches or sometimes a few cents.

When I got towards matric, I started visiting these people in their homes, and arranging outings for them, and parties and suchlike.

But after the mass demonstrations in the city, the police wouldn't leave the Woltemade Centre alone. Every second week they'd bother us and make trouble of one sort or another, and finally, one morning, the offices were raided, and all the papers were taken away. Why, I don't know. Maybe they thought that Adam Pieterse with his no legs was a big threat to the government, or Sissie Williams with her twitching face and spidery arms was about to start a Communist revolution.

One time, my ma and me were on our way to the Cape Flats and we noticed this car tailing us. When we stopped at Mrs Small's place, (she's the one with cerebral palsy), the car stopped behind us. The driver sat in his seat while we got out, keeping his beady eyes fixed on us.

Ma really surprised me. She went up to his window and said 'Excuse me. Why don't you come inside the house and you'll catch me red-handed giving Mrs Small these balls of wool to do her crocheting?'

'Listen here, lady!' the man replied. 'Don't come cheeky with me! Your sort is playing with fire!'

'What do you mean, "my sort"?' Ma asked.

'You'se lot who stir up the troubles with these people.'

'Can't you tell the difference between stirring up trouble and caring for handicapped people?'

'Listen, lady, it's you who must tell the difference. We just keep an eye on you, until you make one wrong move, and then . . . sik-sik!'

As he said 'sik-sik', he pulled his index finger across his neck and stuck the point of his tongue out the side of his mouth, like he was being hanged and having his throat cut at the same time. It didn't look pleasant.

That was when I first realized what sort of trouble a hobby could get you into.

When I turned seventeen I bought an old motorbike that had obviously done the Cape to Cairo route hundreds of times but was still in good shape. Sometimes, no matter where I was going, even if it had nothing to do with the Woltemade Centre, I would see that Sergeant Sik-sik following me. But I had nothing to hide, so what did it bother me, except that it was nerve-wracking to know that every time you stopped to take a leak you were being watched.

Still, it was the same for all the voluntary workers at the Woltemade Centre, even the new girl Grieta, who had recently joined us.

She was working in a bank nearby, but managed to find time to help out regularly at the Centre. Even though she was Afrikaans I got on with her famously. No problems about communication with her. We could have discussed perforations or postmarks till the cows came home, if we were both interested in stamps, which neither of us was.

I got to know her really quite well and discovered that she was doing this voluntary work without her parents' knowledge.

'I couldn't tell my pa,' she told me. 'He would murder me if he knew I was working at such a place.'

'What does your father do?' I asked.

'He's director of this Afrikaans magazine,' she said, 'called *Kaapse Volk*.'

I hadn't heard of it at the time, but since then I discovered it was a very patriotic publication.

'Hey, Grieta,' I said, 'would you care to come with me to Clifton this Sunday?'

I couldn't believe I had asked her.

'Orright,' she said. 'I'd like to.'

I couldn't believe her answer.

She looked fabulous in a swimming costume. She had assets that you wouldn't have guessed from just seeing her at the Woltemade Centre. I mean, her face just seemed to light up in the sunshine, and she looked almost pretty as hell.

We splashed around in the freezing Atlantic waves and played beach tennis and had our picnic of cold chicken and in the evening we went for a meal at the Napoli restaurant in Sea Point.

By the end of the evening we were holding hands and necking. I didn't even care that Sergeant Sik-sik had a good view of us.

It certainly changed the next few months at the Woltemade Centre for me. Grieta and me started hanging out together and we visited the townships together and by the end of three months we were beginning to look like a real couple. Friends who invited one of us around knew that they had to invite both of us. It was a new experience for me. So were a lot of other things that Grieta and me were doing together.

But all this time I never met her parents, until one day she invited me over for a Sunday braai with them.

'Basil, you will have to lie to my dad, hey,' she said.

'Oh, you mean about the Centre?'

'Not only the Centre,' she said. 'You will have to say that we met at college and you will have to try to say a few pro-Afrikaans things, you know what I mean?'

'Of course,' I said, giving her a hug, 'I will tell him that I'm very pro-Afrikaans – I'm very pro-Afrikaans lips, and very pro-Afrikaans kisses, and very pro-Afrikaans . . .'

'That's not what I mean,' she said.

'Don't worry about me,' I said. 'I can handle your dad.'

Well, the braai was fine, and the wine was good, and Meneer and Mevrou de Villiers got on with me just perfectly. I spoke half Afrikaans, half English to them, and they spoke half English, half Afrikaans to me. And I lied about where I met Grieta and they smiled and said how sweet.

After the meal, we all reclined in these fold-out chairs and spoke about the beauty of the Cape and such matters. And the intimate nature of my relationship with the de Villiers scaled new heights when Meneer de Villiers discovered I was a one-time philatelist and began to discuss perforations and postmarks with me.

'Let me show you my collection,' he said, 'if it won't bore you.'

'How can stamps ever bore me?' I said.

He led me to his study, which was furnished with a beautiful stinkwood desk standing on four claw-legs. On the wall were mounted two old Mausers crossing each other, and also the head of an animal which could have been a kudu or a nyala or maybe a gemsbok or an impala – I was never too good on buck.

His collection was all stuck in, of course. He had twelve albums of what he called 'old South Africa' – Cape Colony, Orange River Colony, Transvaal Republic and Natal. But he also had twenty-four albums of mint and first day covers of recent years.

I browsed through his collection admiringly, remarking especially on the fact that he didn't use sticky stamp hinges, but preferred slotting his stamps behind clear plastic.

'Those hinges damage the stamps,' he said. 'I never use them, do you?'

'Never!' I said, which was probably the only thing I said to him all day that wasn't a lie.

Well, after the stamps, I was almost one of the family. After all, I couldn't help being English speaking, and it was possible to be almost a true South African without speaking Afrikaans.

After the visit, my relationship with Grieta got deeper and better. We made good use of the motorbike most nights to drive somewhere elevated, with a view of the city lights or something.

I began to think I was in love for the first time. My thoughts were always of Grieta and I'm sure hers were of me.

It was only natural, with her being female and me being male, that things should take a certain, inevitable course.

So one night we parked the bike in a good spot somewhere near the cablecar station. We found this cosy nook behind some bushes. Then the kissing and cuddling began and the removing of one or two items of clothing that seemed to hamper the natural flow of action between us.

That done, we positioned ourselves very intimately, but very uncomfortably, because unfortunately we did not have a portable double bed.

Now things were hotting up and the barrier between Afrikaans and English was fast disappearing.

'Grieta, ek het jou lief,' I said to her.

'I love you too, Basil,' she said.

I think we'd even forgotten what languages we normally spoke.

I think we'd have forgotten a lot more about ourselves if we'd continued.

But suddenly there was this torchlight flashing on us and revealing parts of Grieta that I didn't even know existed until that moment.

It was that bladdy Sergeant Sik-sik. He peered into our

cosy nook and called out 'Get yourselves decent immediately!'

'Ag, come on Sarge, give us a break!' I shouted out. 'Weren't you young once?'

'I'm counting to ten and then I'm going to come and get you!'

'Okay, Sarge, you're not playing hide and seek. You don't have to count. We'll get decent.'

A few minutes later we came out from the bushes.

'Here we are Sarge, ready-or-not.'

But the smile disappeared fast from my face when I caught sight of someone standing beside Sergeant Sik-sik. It was Meneer de Villiers and he wasn't there to show me first day covers. In his hand was a .45 revolver and it was pointing in a certain general direction – higher than my navel and lower than my throat.

'You bladdy lying Englishman!' he said to me. 'You told me all that crap about Grieta. But you didn't tell me you've changed her into a troublemaker, fraternizing with coloureds, and going into their houses like a Communist, and smoking dagga with them. Sergeant Geldenhuys has told me everything. And now you try to get my girl pregnant and then she will have a half-English bastard child. You stay away from her in future, do you understand! Verstaan jy! If I even see you on the same side of the road as her, you are a dead Englishman.'

He pointed the .45 directly at my face.

'And you, Magriet,' he said, grabbing Grieta painfully by the wrist, 'you're nothing but a slut. You will be locked up from now on. Get in that bladdy car.'

He threw Grieta against the police car and I saw her mouth smack against the metal surface.

My body automatically responded to go and help her, to wipe away the drop of blood forming on her lips. But the .45 moved deliberately into my path.

'You keep away from each other, hear me?'

Grieta climbed into the back of the car, Meneer de Villiers into the front passenger seat. Sergeant Sik-sik stood by the driver's seat for a brief moment before climbing in. I could see his head and shoulders above the roof of the car. He looked over at me in that brief moment, smiled, and then took his index finger and pulled it across his neck and poked the tip of his tongue out the side of his mouth.

Chameleon eyes

When I first started going mad, I don't know.

The idea came to me slowly at first, but then gathered speed as I got to matric and the day of being called up to do army service got nearer.

I used to practise going mad quite a lot.

'My one eye sees one thing, and my other eye sees something quite different,' I used to say.

'What are you talking about, Basil, for God's sake?' my ma would say.

'My one eye sees people, even women and children, with their skulls crushed,' I explained. 'And the other eye sees people having a picnic at Clifton with cold chicken sandwiches.'

I got the idea of going mad from chameleons.

When I was younger and belonged to the Claremont Nature Club, I used to be keen on wildlife. Hyenas, cheetahs, rhinoceroses, warthogs – you name it, I used to know all about them. Not that I ever saw these creatures live, of course, except in the zoo. I probably would have run a mile if a hyena or a warthog came prowling anywhere near me. But I had lots of postcards of these animals.

The only real wildlife I ever came across was ladybugs, lizards, spiders, scorpions and chameleons. Chameleons were my favourite, because you could let them walk up your arm and feed them flies.

A chameleon's tongue is as long as its head and body together – not counting its tail – and this tongue is sticky. It was good fun to put a fly quite far from the chameleon's mouth and watch that tongue shoot out and scoop up its prey.

Another thing you could do with a chameleon was to put it on different coloured objects to see it change colour. It mostly used to work. A chameleon can change from its usual green to a dark reddish grey or to a lighter sort of creamy green – it's something to do with its eyes being sensitive to variations in colour – but personally, I think it changes most when it's afraid.

The weirdest thing of all, though, is the way a chameleon's eyes work. Each moves independently of the other, so that one eye can be fixed on something way over on the left, while the other eye is rolling around looking for something else. It's mad.

'One eye sees people in uniforms beating up and killing other people, the other sees people playing cricket or rugby together at Newlands.'

'You're a bit crazy, you know that, Basil?' my ma would say, putting her palm flat on my forehead to see if I had a raging temperature.

Of course, that one gimmick wasn't going to be enough to persuade anyone other than my ma that I was going loopy.

So I checked our family health book and came up with this illness called schizophrenia, which can even affect adolescents.

'I keep hearing this voice, Ma?'

'Basil, what are you talking about, for God's sake?'

'This man keeps telling me things.'

'What things?'

'He tells me that prison is not the ideal place to spend the next six years.'

'Who tells you this thing?'

'I don't know who he is. I think he's old, maybe my godfather or something.'

'You haven't got a godfather, Basil.'

'Well, he sounds like a godfather. At least he's interested in my life.'

I soon ran out of details from the family health book and went to check books on schizophrenia in the library. What a pity I had burnt the book on the human body which my parents had given me in the hope I would become a doctor! It had a good section on mental illness.

'He talks to me day and night, Ma. I don't know when I'm dreaming any more and when I'm awake. He keeps telling me how horrible prison is.'

'Why does he talk about prison? You're not going to prison.'

'He says I mustn't go to the army either. It's six years in prison for not going.'

'Who has been putting these ideas in your head, Basil? Is it that Jonathan Levy at the Woltemade Centre? I always thought he was too political.'

'No, Ma. Jonathan hardly ever talks to me. It's my godfather.'

'But why doesn't he want you to go to the army, for goodness' sake?'

'Because he doesn't want me to, that's why. He doesn't want me mutilating people's bodies. He wants me to become a priest.'

'What kind of a priest?'

'A Christian priest. He says I would make a good priest or a missionary.'

My ma was not delighted to hear this, as we are supposed to be a Jewish family.

'Are you making this up, Basil?'

'No, Ma, 'strues God I'm not. I wish you could listen in through my one ear, then you'd hear him talking. He's got a loud voice. Do you want to try?'

I don't know what got into me saying something stupid like that. I remember when I was young and Dewie had pins and needles, I said it was contagious.

'You can't catch pins and needles!' Dewie's mother said to me.

'Yes, you can,' I said, and I put my knee against his knee for a few seconds.

'There! I've caught it!' I said. 'My knee's also got pins and needles now.'

Of course, that was ten years ago and even though my ma has a history of depression and she spent a month in a sanatorium after my granny's leg had to be amputated, she wasn't that daft that she'd try and listen to the voice inside my head.

When I stopped eating, my dad started losing patience.

'You better stop this nonsense, Basil. People will say I've got a mad son.'

'What do people matter? None of them are equal,' I said. 'My godfather says I shouldn't live in this world. He says I should go to another world where everyone is equal.'

'You tell your Communist godfather not to put such ludicrous ideas in your head. The only world that meets his description is called Utopia, and that exists only in the minds of lunatics. This here is the real world, you tell your godfather, with real flesh and blood people. And we're all different, but still we have to share the same world somehow, even if a few people get hurt now and then.'

'My godfather says that Utopia sounds like a nice place, even if only lunatics live there.'

'Yes, well you tell your godfather, the way you're going, you'll soon be in a place inhabited only by lunatics.'

'That's a good place for a priest,' I said.

That was when my dad really laid into me. He said he would disown me if I so much as touched the Christian religion with a feather.

Actually, I don't think he mentioned any feathers. I think

I'm getting the memory confused with my cousin, Elise, who used to play doctor–doctor with me and my friend, Rael. Once, when his trousers were down at his ankles, so that he was ready for medical examination, I asked the nurse if she would just give an injection to his private parts. Her answer, if I remember correctly, was: 'What do you think I am, hey? I wouldn't touch those parts of him with a feather.'

Of course, a few years later, it was Elise and Rael who were caught in the bedroom by her father after the matric dance. And she still wasn't using a feather to touch his private parts.

As my madness progressed, I stopped wearing my uniform to school. I wore a red tie with little pink stars instead of the blue and yellow striped tie, and I wore my faded blue denim jacket instead of the navy blue blazer, and I wore broken jeans instead of grey trousers, and Adidas instead of my black schoolshoes.

A few boys laughed when I arrived at school like that and Mr Jarman took me to Mr Tobias's office immediately.

'Where do you think you are, Kushenovitz?' the headmaster said. 'The Coon Carnival?'

'No, sir, but this man said I must dress like this today because of the rotten state of Denmark.'

I got that from reading *Hamlet*. In fact, the whole idea of pretending to go mad and dressing like a weirdo came from *Hamlet*. So please blame Sir William Shakespeare for what was happening to me.

'Was that one of the teachers who told you that?' Tobias asked.

'No! The man who keeps talking to me. He's the one who told me to dress like this. He said you wouldn't mind. He said you'd probably write to the army yourself and tell them that I'm not at all suitable to be a soldier.'

'I always thought you were strange, Kushenovitz, but I didn't know you were round the gramadoelas.'

He phoned my ma to collect me and she took me straight off to Dr Ossip. That's where my studies of schizophrenia really came in handy.

After checking my pulse and looking down my throat and testing my blood pressure and knocking my knees with a rubber hammer, he started asking me questions.

'So when did you last hear this voice?'

'Last night, about 10.15,' I answered. 'Just after I heard the machine guns firing outside in the street.'

'What machine guns?'

'Didn't you hear them?' I thought everyone must have heard them. And especially the tanks.'

'What tanks?'

I started to shake and shiver as I remembered the war going on outside between the South African army and the coloureds and the Indians and the blacks.

'It's alright, Basil,' Dr Ossip said, trying to calm me down.

'They were killing hundreds of people right in front of my eyes. They even crushed the skull of this girl who lives across the road.'

I held my hands up over my eyes to try and forget the vividness of that scene. I bit my lip until it bled and let out this awful primeval groan of agony.

'Calm down, Basil!' Dr Ossip said, but my visions were so vivid.

'My one eye keeps seeing these things. You must tell them I don't want to do their dirty work for them, okay?'

'Alright, Basil, but first let me try to understand. What did the voice actually say to you?'

'He said that I was a special person, chosen specially by him to become a Christian priest or a missionary, and no way should I go into the army. In fact, he said, I should never again wear any uniform. He said uniforms were very dangerous because they stick to your skin and they become part of your skin and you can never take them off afterwards.'

'How long has he been speaking to you?'

'Oh, ever since the war began.'

'When was that?'

'You must know,' I said. 'A long time ago. When I was a kid, and my ears got hurt in the war.'

Dr Ossip was writing notes like mad, and eventually he called my ma into the room and told her that I was terribly tense and probably overstressed from studying for my matric exams and that I probably needed a good rest. He mentioned that my thoughts weren't very coherent and that I was very depressed about the prospect of going into the army to do my military training.

'Do you think he's inherited something from me?' my ma asked.

Poor thing, she wanted to blame herself for my troubles.

'Not at all,' Dr Ossip said. 'You were just depressed. We'll see if Basil gets over this little spell if he relaxes. Take him off for a short holiday. Let him sunbathe – not in the midday sun, of course – and generally take things easy. If there's no improvement in three weeks, bring him back for another checkup. And let him take these tablets. They'll help his body and his mind to relax.'

He handed my ma the prescription.

'By the way,' he said to her, 'did he ever have trouble with his ears when he was young?'

'Yes, he went deaf for about a month when he was two or three years old.'

It wasn't possible for my dad to take time off work to go on holiday, so my ma said she'd just take Ivan and me to the beach everyday.

Of course, the first thing I did, was to substitute aspirin for the tablets Dr Ossip had prescribed for me. And everyday, when my ma asked if I'd taken my pills, I'd answer yes quite truthfully. Once or twice I even made a show of swallowing them in front of her.

But the day of my call-up came ever nearer. I had to go for the army medical checkup and I wasn't looking forward to it at all.

Even thinking of that contact with the army made my head spin.

'Ma, I don't want to be a terrorist.'

'What are you talking about?'

'The army will train me to be a terrorist, to kill and mutilate innocent people.'

My father was not at all impressed.

'Best thing for him would be the army. I did army service and it stood me in good stead all these years. There's nothing like a bit of discipline to straighten out a boy's head.'

'But you didn't have to kill black people, did you?' I screamed at him.

'Who said you'll have to?'

'In the army you have to kill black people and women and children and mutilate their bodies and . . .'

'Jesus, Basil, pull yourself together! You don't have to do any of that. They'll just get you in good physical shape and train you to march and to use a rifle and to survive out in the veld . . .'

'And to cut off people's ears and noses!' I screamed.

After that outburst, I screamed some more, and then again, so that finally my father phoned Dr Ossip and made another appointment for me.

'Has he been taking the tablets?' Dr Ossip asked.

'Yes, he has,' my ma answered.

'And they've had no effect?'

'For the first few days he improved. But now I think he's getting much worse.'

'Well, well, well,' Dr Ossip said. 'I think it's time we had some psychiatric advice on this matter. The man to see is Dr Perlman. He will be able to recommend some form of therapy. But it will be six or eight weeks before you can see him. He's a busy man.'

'I can't wait that long!' I shouted, grabbing hold of the stethoscope that was still hanging round Dr Ossip's neck. 'In six or eight weeks I could be up at the borders, murdering people or I could be in the townships mutilating children, and the uniform could be stuck to my skin and how will I ever get it off?'

But Dr Perlman couldn't be persuaded that I was in urgent need, so it was a seven week wait and therefore the day for the army medical arrived first. There were hundreds of other suckers just like me, but they didn't seem overly perturbed.

This sergeant or whatever he was thought he'd give us a taste of the army in advance and he shouted out his command for us to all get undressed.

'Fully undressed, hey! And that means taking off your filthy underpants, understand?'

I waited in this long queue until I arrived at the desk of the army doctor.

'Basil Kushywhat? Kushewhatthehell? How do you say this name?'

He checked my pulse and looked down my throat and tested my blood pressure and knocked my knees with a rubber hammer. Then he moved to between my legs, squeezed my testicles, and had a good look to check there were two of them, and not one or three, and that I hadn't borrowed anyone else's.

'Ever had polio, scarlet fever, malaria, jaundice, chicken pox, smallpox or letterbox?' he rattled.

'No.'

'Ever had heart trouble? And I don't mean troubles with girlfriends.'

'No.'

'So you're fit and ready to join the army?'

'Yes, perfectly,' I said, 'except for schizophrenia.'

133

'What's wrong with schizophrenia? I tell you, schizo-phrenics make the best lorry drivers in the army.'

'That's okay, then,' I said, 'because a snake loses its skin when it's grown a new one.'

'What's a snake got to do with it?'

'You know,' I whispered, sort of leaning over towards his ear.

'What?'

'When the uniform sticks to me, my old skin will fall off, just like a snake, isn't it? Doesn't it happen to you, sir?'

The army doctor screwed up his nose at me and scruti-nized me.

'Are you trying to make fun of me, Jewboy?'

'No, sir, not in the least, sir,' I said. 'But I'm so worried about sloughing my skin.'

'Sluffing your skin?'

'Yes sir, you know, when my skin falls off. You can't tell yet, though, can you?' I asked him earnestly.

'Tell what?'

'You know, that my snakeskin is falling off. You know the snake even sheds its eyes. I must protect my eyes.'

The army doctor shook his head from side to side, a lopsided smile forming on his lips, as he looked through this folder with my notes on it.

'Your mother's been in a mental home?' he said.

'No.'

'It says here she's been in a sanatorium.'

'That's right,' I said. 'A sanatorium, not a mental home.'

'Shit, man! Don't split hair-ends here with me! She's been in a mental home. And you've been seeing a Dr Ossip about heaving voices. What is this heaving voices shit?'

'Hearing, not heaving,' I explained.

'Oh, hearing voices. What voices?'

'It's nothing,' I said. 'Just my godfather telling me that I must be careful never to cut off anyone's nose or ears. He said it's very unhealthy for me to go round killing and mutilating children. And he also warned me just last night that if I'm not careful with what I wear I could become a coloured or an Indian or even an African. You see, if a chameleon is frightened it can change colour and then it will have to be reclassified.'

'Do you always talk shit like this, or is this something special you save for the army?'

'Oh no, sir, I always talk shit like this. You ask my father. He can't stand it any more. Nor my mother. Nor my brother. And I've got to go and see this Dr Perlman in a few weeks time because he's a psychiatrist and he loves listening to people who talk like me.'

'You're not just putting this on, are you? To get out of military service?'

'No way, sir. It's my godfather who told me that the question is to be or not to be. Because the trouble is my one eye sees things that the other one doesn't see.'

I tried to look in two different directions with each eye.

'You see, my one eye sees only these mutilated bodies.'

I started to shiver and shake at the images of mutilation flashing through my mind. And this unearthly, primeval groan began to escape from my quivering lips.

'But my other eye . . .'

'Liewe hemel! I don't think the army is going to want either of your eyes, Kushywhateveryournameis. Not until you've had some E.C.T. I think some strong electric current in your brain would help your eyes a lot. We will contact your doctor and we will write to you in due course informing you of our decision.'

I tried to control my shaking.

'My godfather will be very pleased with you, sir, except you shouldn't wear that uniform, because it will stick to your skin . . .'

Glossary

ag – an exclamation, similar to the English 'Oh!' (Afrikaans)

amandla – power! (Zulu)

apartheid – separateness (Afrikaans)

ballaboss – big boss (Yiddish)

barmitzvah – Jewish ceremony for the acceptance of a thirteen-year-old Jewish boy into manhood (Hebrew)

bliksem – devilish, roguish (Afrikaans (slang))

bobba – grandmother (Yiddish)

boerewors – thick sausages (Afrikaans)

bokkie – little buck, a term of endearment (Afrikaans)

braaivleis, (*braai*, for short) – barbecue (Afrikaans)

bymekaar – together (Afrikaans)

coloured – (noun) a person of mixed race (South African usage)

Coon – a participant (usually coloured) in the Cape Carnival (formerly the Coon Carnival)

dagga – marijuana (Afrikaans)

dankie – thanks (Afrikaans)

doekie – rag, or scarf worn on the head (Afrikaans)

eina – ouch! (Afrikaans)

ek het jou lief – I love you (Afrikaans)

gramadoelas – wild, remote country (Afrikaans)

Hotnot – disparaging term for a person of Hottentot extraction (Afrikaans)

huis – house (Afrikaans)

Glossary

ja – yes (Afrikaans)

japie – simpleton (Afrikaans)

Joeys – slang for Johannesburg (colloquial)

Kaapse Volk – Cape People (Afrikaans)

knobkierie – wooden club (Afrikaans)

korreltjie – 'peppercorn' hair (Afrikaans)

liewe hemel! – Good heavens! (Afrikaans)

lightie – a young person (colloquial)

Ma Nishtana – a song sung on Passover, asking why this night is different from other nights (Hebrew)

matzah – unleavened bread, like a large cracker biscuit, eaten on the Jewish Passover (Hebrew)

meneer – mister (Afrikaans)

meshugena – mad (Yiddish)

mevrou – missus (Afrikaans)

mos – just (Afrikaans (slang))

nebbish – an insignificant person, a twit (Yiddish)

Nuwejaar – New Year (Afrikaans)

opgeboggered – buggered up (Afrikaans (slang))

oke – a bloke (colloquial)

piccannin (*pikkie*, for short) – European slang for an African child

pondokkie – little hut or shack (Afrikaans)

rand – a unit of South African currency, 100 cents

shochadicke (*shoch*, for short) – derogatory term designating a non-white (Yiddish)

seer – sore (Afrikaans)

sjambok – whip made of dried hide (Afrikaans)

skollie – tramp (Afrikaans)

sommer – casually (Afrikaans)

stoep – verandah (Afrikaans)

stompie – used cigarette stump (Afrikaans)

Sub A – first year of primary school (5/6 year-olds)

velskoen – shoe made of rawhide (Afrikaans)

verstaan – understand (Afrikaans)